FOREST OF SILENCE
Alexis Forrest Mystery
Book 1

KATE GABLE

Byrd Books

Copyright

Copyright © 2023 by Byrd Books, LLC.

All rights reserved.

Proofreader:

Renee Waring, Guardian Proofreading Services, https://www.facebook.com/GuardianProofreadingServices

Cover Design: Kate Gable

No part of this book may be reproduced in any form or by any electronic or mechanical means, including information storage and retrieval systems, without written permission from the author, except for the use of brief quotations in a book review.

This book is a word of fiction. Names, characters, places, and incidents are either products of the author's imagination or are used fictitiously. Any resemblance to actual persons, living or dead, events, or locales is entirely coincidental. The author acknowledges the trademarked status and trademark owners of various products referenced in this work of fiction, which have been used without permission. The publication/use of these trademarks is not authorized, associated with, or sponsored by the trademark owners.

Visit my website at www.kategable.com

Be the first to know about my upcoming sales, new releases and exclusive giveaways!

Want a Free book? Sign up for my Newsletter!

Sign up for my newsletter:

https://www.subscribepage.com/
kategableviplist

Join my Facebook Group:
https://www.facebook.com/groups/
833851020557518

Bonus Points: Follow me on BookBub and Goodreads!

https://www.goodreads.com/author/show/
21534224.Kate_Gable

About Kate Gable

Kate Gable is a 3 time Silke Falchion award winner including Book of the Year. She loves a good mystery that is full of suspense. She grew up devouring psychological thrillers and crime novels as well as movies, tv shows and true crime.

Her favorite stories are the ones that are centered on families with lots of secrets and lies as well as many twists and turns. Her novels have elements of psychological suspense, thriller, mystery and romance.

Kate Gable lives near Palm Springs, CA with her husband, son, a dog and a cat. She has spent more than twenty years in Southern California and finds inspiration from its cities, canyons, deserts, and small mountain towns.

She graduated from University of Southern California with a Bachelor's degree in Mathematics. After pursuing graduate studies in mathematics, she switched gears and got her MA in Creative Writing and English from Western

New Mexico University and her PhD in Education from Old Dominion University.

Writing has always been her passion and obsession. Kate is also a USA Today Bestselling author of romantic suspense under another pen name.

Write her here:

Kate@kategable.com

Check out her books here:

www.kategable.com

Sign up for my newsletter:

https://www.subscribepage.com/ kategableviplist

Join my Facebook Group:

https://www.facebook.com/groups/ 833851020557518

Bonus Points: Follow me on BookBub and Goodreads!

https://www.bookbub.com/authors/kate-gable

https://www.goodreads.com/author/show/ 21534224.Kate_Gable

amazon.com/Kate-Gable/e/B095XFCLL7

facebook.com/KateGableAuthor

bookbub.com/authors/kate-gable

instagram.com/kategablebooks

tiktok.com/@kategablebooks

Also by Kate Gable

**Detective Kaitlyn Carr Psychological
Mystery series
Girl Missing (Book 1)
Girl Lost (Book 2)
Girl Found (Book 3)
Girl Taken (Book 4)
Girl Forgotten (Book 5)
Gone Too Soon (Book 6)
Gone Forever (Book 7)
Whispers in the Sand (Book 8)**

Girl Hidden (FREE Novella)

**Detective Charlotte Pierce Psychological
Mystery series**

Forest of Silence

Last Breath
Nameless Girl
Missing Lives
Girl in the Lake

About Forest of Silence

Forensic psychologist and rookie FBI agent Alexis Forrest returns to her hometown of Broken Hill to investigate the disappearance of a missing teenage girl. Returning to this snowy New England town is the last thing Alexis wants to do. She has a strained relationship with her divorced parents whose relationship did not survive the disappearance and murder of Alexis' older sister, or her dad's prison sentence.

The circumstances of this girl's disappearance are surprisingly similar to her sister's yet the local police aren't exactly welcoming to an inexperienced FBI agent sent to help them solve the case. But then another girl, a wealthy student at a prestigious nearby boarding school, is found dead.

Trying to figure out if the two cases are connected and a serial killer is on the loose, Alexis finds herself getting close to all of the people she thought she had left behind forever. One of those people is a high school boyfriend, a long lost love.

The town is full of secrets that want to stay hidden. To make peace with the past, Alexis must unearth them all. What happens when she finds something that puts her in danger? Will Alexis find who did it or will she become the next victim?

Chapter 1

This was the last place I wanted to be and the first place they told me to go.

I was always what adults described as an observant girl. Wise beyond my years. Always watching, always aware. The kind of quality that helped earn me a place in the FBI. I saw what others didn't. I was content to let the people around me take the spotlight while I stood behind them, observing.

So it's no big surprise when I return to my hometown for the first time in three years and find it just as divided as ever. As I cross the border into Broken Hill, I'm surrounded by small, sometimes ramshackle homes. In spring and summer, when the trees are full of leaves and the grass is green, it can be pretty out here.

At this time of year, on the other hand? A thin layer of snow coats nearly everything, washing out the color, and the bare limbs that sway gently in the breeze remind me of bony fingers reaching for the sky. A cloudy sky, flat and gray, which only lends to the sense of foreboding. A scrawny dog lopes down the street, lifting its leg and dyeing a patch of snow yellow before moving on. Charming.

It's only a few minutes of driving before the quality of the homes and the cars parked in front of them begins to improve. That's Broken Hill in a nutshell. It starts out sort of grim and sketchy along the outskirts but becomes comfortable and even affluent the further one travels. Here, the streets have been carefully plowed, unlike the slushy mess I rolled through at first. Instead of single story shacks and doublewides, there are modest but quaint single family homes arranged neatly along tree lined streets. I know that they looked dazzling just a month ago when the leaves had burst out in all their colorful glory. The sightseers arrived on schedule, no doubt, jamming up the bed and breakfasts in the heart of town, and generally irritating the locals. The fact that these peepers inject tons of cash into the town's economy doesn't seem to matter as much to the residents as the disturbance of their peace.

Around here, that's what it's all about. Customs. Tradition. Working hard and paddling your own canoe. Typical New England determination at its finest.

I see through it now. The stark difference in class, so obvious when you're coming into town but maybe not as clear when you've spent your life inhabiting it. For most of my early childhood, I grew up blissfully unaware of the poverty on the outskirts of this place. But since my family were squarely middle class, I was also sure never going to attend Hawthorne Academy, the expensive boarding school nestled in the heart of town like a jewel tucked away in a velvet box. Broken Hill High was more my speed.

Still for a little while there, we lived well in the rambling Victorian my parents never did manage to remodel into the bed and breakfast they'd once dreamed of. That was back when they dreamed. Back when they shared a life.

Back before everything fell to pieces.

I check the clock on the dash and snicker. I've been in town for less than ten minutes, and that's where my thoughts headed. How could they not? Everywhere I look, there's a memory that's somehow been ruined by the cloud that's hung over my family for two decades. When I pass the courthouse on Main Street I have to avert my gaze while my stomach tightens and my heart flutters in my chest. It's almost enough to make me pull over and catch my breath, but I have people waiting for me. When I reach a red light I force myself to inhale deeply and let it out slowly. I am not going to let the past get in the way of what needs to be done.

Somebody needs me.

Somebody I can actually help this time.

I hope.

If I looked up the word *idyllic* in the dictionary, it wouldn't surprise me to find a picture of what I now roll through at a reduced speed—this is a busy, bustling part of town, and drivers who don't heed the fifteen mile an hour speed limit end up paying handsomely for being in a hurry. When you rely on tourist dollars the way Broken Hill does, you have to accommodate the public, meaning there's no speeding through the town's commercial district if you don't want to run over a jaywalker. A handful of boutique hotels have popped up in the years since my last visit, while *No Vacancy* signs hang in front of gingerbread Victorians that look almost heart-breakingly beautiful with a touch of snow frosting their roofs and the well-manicured trees and shrubs. It's like something out of a postcard, something Norman Rockwell might have painted.

But just underneath the idyllic surface is a deeper truth. The sort of truth I might never have grasped if it hadn't been for that night. The night we never talk about. The night that managed to leave a footprint on our lives. No matter how we avoid talking about it, it's always there, always in the middle of everything. It changed the landscape of our existence.

I have to force the memories deep down inside once I've reached the police station a few blocks from the courthouse. Like nearly all of the buildings in this part of town, it's a stately, brick structure set behind a wide set of marble steps that freeze over right on schedule every winter. I have to chuckle to myself when I find a man in uniform sprinkling rock salt along their surface. Some things never change.

But I have.

I take a look at myself in the mirror once I've parked in the lot beside the building and I'm almost surprised to find a thirty-year-old woman gazing back at me. Something about being here takes me back to days that should have been simpler and sweeter and might have been if fate hadn't stuck her nose in the middle of everything (if you believe that sort of thing). There's open, frank worry in my hazel eyes and fine brackets at the corners of my full mouth. I'm a little young for wrinkles, but there's no arguing my reflection. I've been dreading this trip from Boston ever since I got word that I was being sent up here. You don't argue with your superiors, especially when you're a rookie agent in your first year with the Bureau.

To my boss, this was a no brainer. I know this town, I know the way people think around here. Sure, I wanted to throw myself on my knees and beg him to send anybody else, literally anyone, but that was only my immediate reaction. By the end of the day, I saw how much sense it makes. And by the following morning, it occurred to me that I might be able to help another family avoid what mine had suffered. I mean, why else did I get into this career in the first place?

I'm quick to run my fingers through my light brown locks before pulling them back into a ponytail. After smoothing down a few fly-aways,

Forest of Silence

I take a deep, bracing breath and open my door… before recoiling in frozen horror. It can get cold as hell in Boston, but there's something about late autumn in Maine that can steal the air from a person's lungs if they're not prepared. I knew it was going to be colder, but I forgot the particular chill in the air, especially when there's snow on the ground. Even the most innocent breeze can turn frigid, and that's what I'm dealing with as I climb out of the car and navigate the parking lot on foot. There are still icy, slushy patches here and there, but I've managed them with ease before climbing the salty steps and entering the station.

Time to meet the task force.

The desk cop positioned near the entrance lifts an eyebrow when I appear in front of him. I raise my badge, hanging from a lanyard around my neck. "High, there. Agent Alexis Forrest. I'm here to meet with Captain Christopher Felch about the Martin case."

There's no getting around announcing my affiliation. I'm prepared for the disdainful look I get, along with a few muffled snorts from the cops a little further back in the bullpen.

"Well, well." The cop— Officer Fisher, according to the name badge— leans back in his chair and folds his arms. "Aren't we lucky? The Bureau decides to send its prettiest agent to help us do our job."

His words drip in New England drawl; all nasal and full of dropped r's.

Your job? You sit behind a desk and direct people when they come in. Right. Because that would earn me any points. "Can you show me where I can find Captain Felch?"

"Don't fret. He'll find you." And with that, he rotates away from me in his chair, sharing a laugh with his buddies.

So much for cooperation. But that's fine. I'm not here to make friends— and even though I think it might earn me points, I don't see any need to announce that I grew up here.

As it turns out, I don't have to. "Hey, I know who you are."

My head snaps up and I look around before realizing the tall, grinning man is talking to me. He strides my way wearing a big, goofy grin. His golden blond hair gleams in the overhead lights while his blue eyes sparkle. Mr. All-American Boy.

"Me?" I ask.

"Sure."

"And who are you?"

"Andy Cobb, Agent Forrest." He glances around like he's making sure others are paying attention, and there's a sick feeling in my stomach that only gets worse once he continues. "You're the one whose sister was murdered all those years ago, right? And your dad shot the guy on the courthouse steps."

Well, there it is. It was bound to come out eventually, though I didn't figure it would be as loud and obnoxious and generally embarrassing. All at once, everyone's attention shifts to me, and I might as well be ten years old again.

The girl whose sister was murdered.

The girl whose father went to prison for trying to kill the man convicted.

For the next eight years after the terrible night we lost Maddie, I got used to the whispers. The funny looks, the sympathetic frowns. In the twelve years since, I sort of lost the thick skin I built up.

There's no choice but to lift my chin and get through it, because this won't be the last time someone brings up the past and I'd better get used to it. Yet before I can offer a reply, a tall, middle-aged man claps his hands sharply and draws the attention of everyone in the vicinity.

"Let's go. Conference room." His narrowed

gaze sweeps over the room and everyone gathered in it. "It's time for a briefing on the Martin case."

Something tells me I just got my first look at Captain Felch.

Chapter 2

"Agent Forrest." Captain Felch has a strong grip that he demonstrates when he shakes my hand. "I wish I could say it's a pleasure."

"I understand." As we chat, the room fills with officers who chatter quietly settling in around a long table. Those who can't find a chair line up along the walls. I don't think there's a single one who doesn't give me a look that I would describe as unwelcoming if I were feeling generous. Really, they're flat-out hostile for the most part. I am the living, breathing reminder that somebody somewhere doesn't think they have what it takes to find a missing girl.

Once everyone's gathered, the captain clears his throat. "Everyone, this is Agent Alexis

Forrest. She's our FBI liaison from the Boston office, and she'll be helping us investigate Camille Martin's case."

There's a brief ripple that goes over the room. A few of them— women, all— nod in greeting. Not the men. They would rather sneer and look offended. That's fine. They wouldn't be the first.

Pinned to a corkboard spanning the wall behind us is a blown-up photo which the captain points to. "Camille Martin. Fifteen-year-old sophomore at Broken Hill High. Her parents are both teachers there, and they're convinced she would never have run away. Somewhere between her shift over at *Broken Hill Books and Coffee* and the time she was expected to arrive at the family home, something happened. It's up to us to figure out what."

Beside the photo of the smiling, dark-haired kid, there's a map. "The family's home sits just here." He points to a spot I vaguely recognize as the area I drove through between the trailer park and downtown. Middle class, maybe a little on the poorer side. If both parents earn a high school teacher's salary, I can imagine why. "It's around two miles from the bookshop. Camille was supposed to get a ride, according to the

24

store's owner, but she assured him she could walk. From the way he tells it, her shift ended at five-thirty and the café closed at nine-thirty. It was only the two of them working, meaning he would have had to close the shop to drive her home. The snow fell earlier that day, but it had stopped by then, the wind had died down, and she was sure she could make it easily. As we know now, she never made it home."

He releases a heavy sigh. "That was more than forty-eight hours ago. The only two surveillance cameras set up facing the street happen to be out of order now." A soft groan rises around me. "The rest of the cameras face inside, monitoring customers. All we have is this from the store owner."

He picks up a remote and points it at the laptop set up on the conference table. The image appears on a screen spanning the wall to my left, with a timestamp that reads *5:47 PM*. I recognize Main Street easily, even though the image covers a narrow area. Through the front door emerges the girl in the photo.

Camille.

She's pretty, fresh-faced, smiling when she looks back into the store like she's saying good-bye. She's dressed in a dark polo shirt that I assume was provided by her boss, jeans, and sneakers. She finishes zipping up her puffy jacket and crams a knit hat over her dark tresses, then starts walking with her shoulders hunched like she's trying to adjust to the cold.

Camille. What happened to you?

"We've been through her cell and her laptop. We've combed through her social media. There's still information to be uncovered, but as far as we know from preliminary interviews, she had no plans to meet up with anyone."

I'm like a kid in school, raising my hand slightly to get his attention. "Any family or friends seem withholding or suspicious?"

"They couldn't be more cooperative. Everyone we've spoken to thinks the world of this kid, and they all want to see her come home."

Not to attract even more attention, but I have another question. "You mentioned looking through her phone. Do we have it?"

"We," somebody mutters while someone else snickers.

Captain Felch shoots them a dirty look over the top of my head, and the snickering ends. "We accessed her iCloud account. Her laptop was still at home, but she had her phone on her.

It's missing." Then, like he's anticipating the next natural question, he adds, "Conveniently— or inconveniently, depending on how you look at it— the Find My iPhone feature was turned off."

Of course it was. Now I understand why he looks so tired, almost pained. Girls go missing all the time, and there are no obvious leads so far.

Just like another case I was unfortunately connected to.

My first stop is the most obvious one. Camille was last seen at the bookstore, so that's where I'm headed, walking the couple of blocks rather than taking the car. After sitting in that stifling station with so much judgment bearing down on me, it's a relief to get outside. The air is so cold it burns my lungs, but I welcome the sensation. It centers me.

The first word that comes to mind as I approach the shop is *charming*. Almost annoyingly so. Just like downtown Broken Hill is a postcard of a quintessential New England town, the bookshop is similarly picturesque. There are books arranged in windows outlined in white twinkle lights and decorated with paper snowflakes. A distinct scent of old paper and coffee envelopes me as soon as I open the door.

This isn't the time to take a deep, relaxing breath. I still do for some reason. I've always been a bookworm, and the sight of a small fireplace with a pair of leather chairs arranged in front of it does something to me. All I'd need is a thick blanket and an even thicker book, and I'd be set for the rest of the day. The shelves practically bow under the weight of so many books in every conceivable genre, all of which are listed on cheerful cards taped at the ends of the rows.

"Can I help you find something, ma'am?"

At the sound of that deep voice, I turn away from a row of biographies to find a friendly, smiling face. A smiling face that's much too familiar.

I never did get the owner's name, did I? I was in too much of a hurry to escape the heavy, hostile energy at the station.

Now, I'm staring at my past once again.

"Mitch? Mitch Dutton?" Strange how a name that was once as familiar as my own now threatens to get stuck in my throat.

He looks the same as before. It's almost as if not a day has passed since the last time we set eyes on each other. His light gray turtleneck sets off ice-blue eyes I'd spent hours gazing into in a former life, while his chocolate-brown hair looks as thick and soft as ever. Good thing my hands are in my coat pockets, or else he'd see the way they flex into fists as I fight the urge to reach out and brush a few strands away from his eyes.

His smile. Jesus, it's as heart-stopping as ever. Maybe more so, since he's no longer a teenage boy. He's a man. "Alexis. Holy crap. What brings you here?"

Before I can answer or even suck in a breath, his smile slips away. "Of course. Stupid question."

My attempt at a friendly-if-bewildered grin turns into something closer to a grimace. "You know what I do for a living?"

"What? You think my high school girlfriend left town and I never asked about her?" He lowers his brow, shooting me a knowing look. "Your mom stops in on occasion. She says it's because she's addicted to my cinnamon rolls, but I get the feeling she likes bragging about her daughter."

Lies. She's never bragged about me. Whatever warm, maternal feelings she possessed died with Maddie. But he's trying, and I have to meet him halfway. "She didn't tell me you're working here, but then we don't speak all that often."

"I don't work here. I own the place."

"You do?"

His head bobs up and down, but his jaw tightens like he's in pain. "I should've closed for a few minutes. I shouldn't have let her go."

The agent in me watches this like an outsider, coolly observing his behavior and making note of the pain in his voice.

The ex-girlfriend in me wants to offer comfort. I can't do that. Not yet, at least. I'm here on business. "It's easy to blame ourselves when something awful happens. I'm sure Camille took that walk dozens of times and made it home just fine."

"Thanks." He straightens his posture a little and lifts his heavy brows. "So, what can I do for you, Agent Forrest?"

Captain Felch already announced the store's owner was plainly visible in the store's security footage and that he locked up at nine-thirty, four hours after Camille left the shop. The chances of him being a suspect are slim to none. My relief is palpable. "What can you tell me about

Camille? Did it seem like she was hiding something? Or maybe like she was excited or nervous?"

He shakes his head. "She's a sweet kid, hardworking. She cut out the snowflakes on the window and hung the lights. Usually, a high school kid takes an afterschool job and they show up and do the bare minimum. But she engages with the customers and takes her work seriously. I was planning to offer her full-time hours over winter break and again over the summer."

He speaks about her in the present tense. He has hope. My heart softens while I ask myself why I couldn't have put on a little more makeup today. I wanted to look professional when I met the task force. Nobody told me I'd run into an old boyfriend. I consider letting my hair out but I don't want to look like I'm trying too hard to make an impression.

"We're going to do everything we can," I assure him, though I know damn well the odds aren't in our favor. Two days have passed, and every minute that ticks by makes it less likely we'll find her alive.

"I know you will. Nobody's more tenacious than you."

"You haven't known me in a long time."

His eyes twinkle as he shakes his head. "Not you. You wouldn't change."

Neither has he. He's just as charming as ever. It's almost enough to make me question why we broke up in the first place. But it was a wise decision made by two stupid teenagers. I was going to Boston University and he was staying local and attending the University of Maine. We didn't want things to be complicated.

Mitch checks out a few customers so I hang back and watch out of the corner of my eye while exploring the shop. The front half is devoted to books, while the back is where coffee and pastries are sold. A handful of small tables sit scattered between the café counter and the bookshelves, where people can sit and read while drinking coffee.

"What do you think?" Mitch asks once we're alone.

"I think it's adorable and cozy and the sort of place I'd love to spend an afternoon."

He rocks back on his heels, jamming his ring-free hands into his jeans pockets and grinning, in that familiar bashful way that used to turn my heart to a puddle. "You feel like sharing that review on Yelp?"

For the first time today, I laugh, and he joins me. "I'll get on that. Well, I'd better get moving." There's regret behind my announcement, but I am here for a reason that doesn't involve flirting or reconnecting with an old flame. "I only rolled in this morning, so I haven't yet met the parents."

His expression hardens slightly. "They're really distraught," he says and I can almost taste his sorrow. "Why don't I give you my card in case you have any other questions?"

I have to fight off a knowing grin when he snatches a card from a small display on the counter. "I'll keep this close by," I assure him before tucking it into my coat and trying to ignore how thrilling it was when our hands brushed.

But now is not the time. There's a girl out there somewhere, and I need to focus entirely on that.

Chapter 3

Some things never change. How many times have I heard that little gem? Coming back home is proof enough of how true that is. There might be new businesses in town, and I drove past two different construction sites on my way to Broken Hill High. Condos, it looks like. Little villages nestled in the heart of a larger village. Time hasn't completely stopped.

But when it comes to the town's public high school, time may as well have stood still. Not only for the past three years since my last visit, but in the twelve years since I graduated. I could easily be parking before class as I pull in, though now I'm in the faculty lot as a visitor. So many memories of what had been came crashing down at once. It's one thing for my presence in town to stir to life so much of what I've tried to squash down and forget. It's another to stare up at the three-story brick building and fight through the sensation of a tidal wave sweeping over me, pulling me down into dark water I haven't dipped a toe in for more than a decade.

But this isn't about me. I remind myself of that as my heavy soled shoes crunch over a film of ice that's formed on top of the snow-covered lawn. This is about Camille. The clock is ticking.

I know the way to the front office by heart, hanging a right after climbing the same fifteen granite steps I climbed every morning on my way into the building. Scent is so evocative. It has the power to immerse us in the past before we know what's happening. The smell of the floor polish is almost enough to knock me back a few steps once I'm inside the front lobby, but I push through, ignoring the curious glances of a pair of giggling students leaving the office before I step inside.

My God, even this is the same, right down to a few of the ladies chatting over their coffee. I clear my throat to get their attention.

"Good morning. I'm Agent Alexis Forrest, and I've been assigned the Camille Martin case.

I was hoping to speak to Mr. and Mrs. Martin, and I understand they're here today." Frankly, I can't imagine why. If my kid went missing a few days ago, the last place I'd want to be is work. Especially if it meant being surrounded by a bunch of kids her age, kids she grew up with.

"Of course, I remember you." I vaguely recognize the woman who speaks, thanks in part to the fact that her hairstyle hasn't changed since I graduated. I don't think it's changed since the late nineties—she uses enough hair-spray on her mile-high bangs to keep an entire company in business.

What do you remember? The student, or the girl whose sister was killed? I force my way through a smile instead of asking that ugly question. "Yes, Mrs. Baker, I remember you as well. It's nice to see you. The circumstances could be better."

Her eyes cloud over with sadness that seems to be shared by the rest of the group. Her voice drops closer to a whisper as she explains, "Brian and Tess are probably in the faculty lounge. They have substitutes handling their classes, and they've been camped out in there all morning."

Interesting. "Thank you. I know the way," I tell the ladies, all of whom chortle softly.

The faculty lounge is on the second floor,

meaning I climb a flight of stairs in a narrow stairwell, thankful that there are classes going on. Otherwise, I'd get caught up in the flow of traffic as everyone hurries to their next class. In such a large building— the length of two football fields, if I remember correctly— every second counts. In my junior year, I had to make it from the school's gym at one end of the building all the way to the opposite end for psychology in the auditorium. It's amazing I didn't break my neck sprinting down the hall, getting jostled and bouncing off one backpack after another.

Granted, I would have had a little extra time if I weren't busy making out with Mitch after we got changed out of our gym clothes, but that's another story. That's how kids are. Every second I could spend with him, I was by his side. No question. I can almost taste the mint gum he used to chew nonstop back then. He confessed once that he did it to keep his breath fresh for me.

Not the time, Alexis. This trip isn't supposed to be a fun little walk down memory lane. I'll have all the time in the world to think about Mitch once we find Camille.

The teacher's lounge sits between the girls

and boys bathrooms halfway along the school's west wing. Across the hall is the computer lab. I can hear the typing going on in there, while the sound of faint music floats down the hall from orchestra practice. I wonder how many of the kids under this roof are thinking of Camille now. I wonder if it's hard for them to concentrate.

I knock at the closed door before easing it open. The last thing these people need is somebody barging in on them. They are hard at work, and now I understand why they're here and not at home. They're using the copiers to make posters. Judging by the neat piles already arranged along a table that sits against the far wall, they've been at it all morning.

Mr. Martin notices me first. He's still as good looking as I remembered him, without so much as a hint of gray in his sandy hair. Plenty of girls had crushes on him back in the day. He was the kind of charismatic teacher who engaged his students. He didn't try too hard to be everybody's buddy. His naturally friendly, warm personality shone through. I was always sorry I never had his English class.

His wife, on the other hand, I remember very well. She turns when I clear my throat, and it's like looking at her daughter. Camille inherited her mother's shining dark hair and delicate features, plus the wide, coffee-colored eyes that are now terribly bloodshot and swollen. They both look like they threw on whatever wrinkled clothes they could find this morning. Tess's sweater is inside out. I doubt she'd care if she knew.

"Mr. and Mrs. Martin," I begin softly, offering a sympathetic smile. "I don't know if you remember me. I'm Alexis Forrest, and I now work with the FBI. I've been assigned Camille's case."

"Please. Brian and Tess." Brian extends a hand which I shake firmly before turning to his wife.

Light flares to life behind her eyes. "Of course, I remember you. AP Psychology, right?"

"That's right. I'm surprised you remember me."

"You were one of my favorite students." She barks out an almost silent laugh. "That's the sort of thing teachers tell their old students all the time, but I mean it with you."

"To tell you the truth, I loved your class so much that I ended up studying for my PhD in forensic psychology down at the University of

Virginia. That was my last stop before the FBI. You inspired me."

"That is so nice to hear." She's been smiling for too long. Now it cracks before the light drains from her eyes. "I'm sorry. I'm ... very tired. Do you know anything? Have you heard anything new?"

"Captain Felch gave me a full rundown. I only arrived in town a couple of hours ago." I nod toward a cluster of chairs near a window overlooking the snow-covered football field. "Can we sit down? I promise, I won't take too much of your time."

Brian sits, propping his head on his palms, elbows on his knees. He's the picture of a grieving father. Tess sits beside him and leans against him, letting her cheek touch his shoulder. Now I remember when Camille was born. God, it's surreal, thinking back to when the beloved Mrs. Martin went out on maternity leave. She used to talk about Camille every so often during class, too. And now I'm here to investigate her disappearance.

"I'm only going to ask a few questions, and I'm sorry if they've been asked before. I'm sure you don't like having to repeat yourself."

Forest of Silence

"It's no problem," Tess whispers. "It might help somehow."

I pull out my phone and open the audio recording app. After making note of the date and time, I launch into my first questions. "What can you tell me about her? What did she do after school? Who was she friends with? Did she have any hobbies?"

"I'll tell you exactly what I told the police; Camille is a good girl." Brian lifts his head, staring at me with eyes so full of pain I want to look away from them. But I can't. I won't. The least I can do is face him and let him know I'm not going to run away. "Straight A's. Conscientious. Plenty of friends."

"And you knew her friends?"

"You know how it is around here," Tess murmurs. "Everyone knows everybody else. These kids, they've grown up in front of us."

"She always hung out with good kids," Brian assures me. "The kind of teenagers you know are going to make something of themselves one day. Like you were."

"Did she ever stay out late?"

They shake their heads in unison. "She was always home by curfew. If she were spending the night somewhere, one of us would talk to

41

the parents to confirm. There was no sneaking around."

On one hand, I'm glad to hear it. On the other, I'm not coming up with many leads based on their descriptions. Surely, Camille can't be this perfect.

What if she is? Too often nowadays, kids end up getting mixed up with the wrong people, usually online. You don't have to break curfew to meet a predator over the internet. "What about her browsing habits? You know kids today and their phones."

"Are you kidding? I tried to take a phone away from one of the kids a few weeks ago and I would swear he was about to have a seizure." But Brian shrugs his shoulders anyway. "She never fought us on turning that thing off when it came time for homework or dinner."

"Believe me," Tess adds. "As teachers, we have to stay on top of the latest trends and threats. What to look for, that sort of thing. If anything, we've been hypervigilant. There were no warning signs."

"She did date a boy last year," Brian murmurs while his wife fishes a tissue from her pocket to wipe her leaking eyes. It's not that she's actively crying— she's able to clearly answer my questions— but the tears roll down her cheeks just the same. "They broke up, but it was very low drama. Camille is not a dramatic girl."

Now we're getting somewhere. "What's his name?"

"Danny Clifton. Decent kid, never any trouble," Brian reports. "Otherwise, we even suggested she date somebody new. With the Soph Hop coming up at the end of the year, we figured it might be nice for her to have a date."

"But she's never very interested," Tess concludes. "Always studying. Pulling shifts at the bookstore to save up money."

"I have one more question, and then I'll leave you to it here. I understand there's a press conference at one o'clock, down at the police station."

Tess nods. "That's right. After that, we want to start papering the town with these signs."

"Did she ever mention anything about anyone following her around? This could be anybody. Customers at the store, kids at school, anyone."

They both wear the same blank look, shrugging. "Never."

"Would you mind giving me the names of

her friends so I can talk to them?" Tess rattles off a handful of names which I make note of before standing and offering them a sympathetic smile. "I'll see you at the station. I'm going to do everything I can."

Now, all I have to do is to find something.

Chapter 4

Captain Christopher Felch is the sort of man who looks like he's seen it all. He's got the grim sort of determination that I respect. He doesn't need to strut around the station like a peacock, reminding everybody who's in charge. He doesn't bully. He doesn't shout or threaten.

I find him sitting at his overflowing desk when I return from my visit with the Martins. I stopped and grabbed a sandwich along the way, knowing there wouldn't be much time to worry about eating otherwise. "Do you mind?" I ask, pulling the wrapped sandwich from a paper bag.

"By all means. Is that from Nick's?"

"Where else? They still make the biggest sub in town." And one bite tells me it's still the best.

I was too nervous about the trip to have break-fast, so this couldn't come at a better time.

"What are your impressions?"

I swallow a big bite and take a swig of iced tea before answering. "She's a good kid."

"It seems that way." He runs a hand over his salt and pepper hair, cropped close. He wears a wedding band on his left hand, and there are framed photos of small kids and a smiling woman on the credenza behind him. A family man. I wonder how personally he takes a case like this.

"She seems happy, well-adjusted, and conscientious. This doesn't look like a runaway."

"Agreed. She's not the type."

"After I left the school, I swung back around to the bookstore and drove the most logical route she would have walked to get home." I grab a napkin to dab some mayonnaise that dripped onto my chin before continuing. "There was plenty of opportunity for somebody to grab her. At this time of year, and with the sky being overcast like it was that day, it was pretty dark for hours."

I can see it in my head, having only driven through there minutes ago. "Lots of woods. Long driveways. Houses set far enough back from the road that it makes sense, nobody seeing anything out of the ordinary. Most of the houses aren't even visible from the road."

"What does that tell you?"

"It tells me anything could have happened. It tells me if somebody picked her up, they chose that area to do it in because they knew the chance was good that they'd get away with it."

He nods slowly, his brows pinching together like he's in pain. "That's what we've been wrestling with."

"I would still like to interview all the people living along that route."

"Even though their homes are too far from the road to see anything?"

"I want to know if they have cameras pointed toward the road."

"Why would they do that?"

"It's extremely common nowadays. Doorbell cameras, that sort of thing. And I noticed one of the mailboxes was broken like somebody took a baseball bat to it." I have to push away a laugh when countless memories come flooding back. I never would have done it myself, but I knew plenty of kids who did. "I mean, what is the point of knocking down mailboxes? I never did figure that out."

"I'd like to know the answer to that, myself."

"People like to install these cameras nowadays so they can keep an eye on things. Plus, you know, with Amazon deliveries being so common —and people stealing packages from porches..."

"Gotcha. I didn't think about that since the houses are so far away from the road." And he looks annoyed with himself, which I guess I would be, too. I'd remind him that's why I'm here, to think about the things he and his force might have missed, but there's no need to rub it in.

"Go ahead, Agent. Hopefully we'll get lucky." He picks up a coffee cup and sniffs it like he's trying to figure out how long it's been sitting out. "I guess I don't have to tell you how damn frustrating it is, a case like this. A girl ups and vanishes into thin air. That sort of thing's not supposed to happen in this day and age, with the technology we have."

I have to force myself to breathe through the tightness in my chest. Right on schedule. He doesn't even have to be talking about Maddie, but it's Maddie who flashes in my memory. Her smile, her laugh. She was such a good sister. I could go to her with anything and know she'd keep my secret. She was no narc. And she never tried to lord over me that she was the big sister, like I had to listen to everything she said or else. Not even close.

I didn't realize I'd drifted off until the Captain clears his throat. "Cameras will start arriving soon. I'd better splash my face, try to look half human before they get here." I take that as my cue to stand and leave his office, but he shakes his head and motions for me to stay put. "Until we have your office set up, feel free to stay here. Go over your notes, whatever it is you need to do. I'll let you know when it's time for the press conference to start."

I understand they're going to stick me in an unused office that turned into storage after a while. Either nobody thought to clean it out for me, or they're deliberately dragging their feet to make me as uncomfortable as possible. As if we aren't all on the same team. But to them, we're not. By now, they all know I was born and raised here, yet that doesn't seem to make a difference.

They hold my affiliation with the Bureau against me. I only hope this doesn't end up hurting the investigation.

By the time I've listened to the recording I made with the Martins and jotted down my impressions, there's a rap against the glass wall looking out over the desks beyond the office. Captain Felch crooks his finger and I hop up, hurrying out to join him in the conference room. The table that was in the center of the room earlier has been pushed against the wall to make room for the dozen or so reporters snapping photos and taking notes while they wait for the Martins to make a statement.

The bulletin board has been stripped of the photos and maps that were on it only hours ago, replaced by a single, blown-up poster. It's the same image the Martins used in the flyers they were copying earlier. The image I studied this morning was a carefully posed yearbook photo, but this is a more natural shot. Camille sits cross-legged beside a wrapped box, and in her arms she holds a puppy with a bow around its neck. A birthday gift? She's beaming from ear to ear, fresh faced, full of joy. If I remember correctly, she turned fifteen over the summer. I'm sure the dog misses her like crazy.

At one on the dot, Captain Felch steps to the front of the room, standing to the right of the poster. He makes a few remarks, mostly pertaining to the respect he hopes everyone shows the Martins. "They will not be answering any questions," he explains. "But they plan to share information about their daughter which they would like the public to know. The intent here is to raise awareness, not to pry into their lives or ask leading questions which might upset them. I hope all of you will respect them at this terrible time."

He looks over my head and waves someone forward, and the silence that falls over the room tells me the Martins have arrived before I look over my shoulder for confirmation. They've changed from the sloppy clothes they wore earlier and are now dressed neatly, conservatively. But there's no hiding the pain etched on both their faces as they step up in front of their daughter's poster.

"Thank you to everyone for taking the time to be here today." Brian's voice is thick with emotion. He clears his throat before continuing. "As you know, our daughter, Camille, went missing more than seventy-two hours ago while on her way home from her after-school job. We are doing everything we can to bring her home, and both local law enforcement as well as the FBI have been nothing but generous with their resources. Still, Camille is missing. It's becoming clearer that someone took her from us."

"Camille is not the sort of girl who would run away from home," Tess insists in a flat, no-nonsense voice. Like she's answering the inevitable question that's sure to come to everyone's minds. "She has been the light of our lives from the minute she was born, and we've been nothing but proud of her every day of her life. She is a beloved friend, a hard-working student, the sort of girl who never misses a shift and is always home before curfew. And we want her back."

I have to grind my teeth together to will away the overwhelming emotion that threatens to choke me. It wouldn't exactly look professional if I burst into tears, but there's no denying how heartbreaking this is. These are good people. They devote their lives to teaching kids and while I've never looked at their pay stubs I'm going to guess they don't make nearly what they deserve. They work hard. They change lives for the better.

And now they're living through the same nightmare my parents faced.

I really hope they manage to get through this together. My parents certainly didn't.

Chapter 5

"What, are you trying to show everybody up by being the last one out of here?"

I look up from my notes to find Andy Cobb — the cop who outed me to the rest of the department— smirking from the doorway to my makeshift office. It's a little cramped, and there are still boxes stacked in one corner, but it will do for now.

I'm too startled to form a response. "Excuse me?" I was deep in thought, jotting down questions I want to ask Camille 's friends once I get a few minutes with them. The ex-boyfriend, too. He's a natural lead, even if the two of them haven't dated since last year. I have already been through his social media accounts. He's a handsome kid and seems to have a lot of friends. But plenty of people are skilled at hiding their dark sides. I wonder if he's one of them.

Andy jerks his chin toward the desk I was hunched over only a moment ago. "I'm saying you are already the star around here, Agent. You don't have to rub it in by staying late. There's no extra credit points for that."

"Who said I'm interested in extra credit points?" Folding my arms, I look him straight in the eye. Big surprise— he looks away, and his naturally ruddy complexion darkens.

"I was only busting your balls. But seriously, it's late. You don't need to burn yourself out on the first day." He touches two fingers to his temple in a makeshift salute, then strolls off, whistling to himself.

The fact is, I lost track of time. It's past six-thirty. My eyes go wide, even if losing time is nothing new for me. When I'm in the zone, everything else tends to melt away.

He does make a good point, even if he's clumsy as hell about it. I roll my head from side to side to loosen up my stiff neck before blowing out a heavy sigh. I've been dreading this. Some people might look forward to heading out at the end of a long, almost brutal day, and I might be one of them if I looked forward to what happens next.

The idea of getting a room at some cheap motel is painfully attractive as I leave the station. Right away I gather my coat collar in my fist, closing it tight in hopes of warding off the bitter cold that's settled in now that darkness has fallen. An icy breeze cuts straight through the heavy wool anyway, forcing me to hustle to the car. I keep meaning to price automatic starters, so the heat can be running by the time I climb in. Instead, I shiver and blow into my cupped hands while waiting for the heater to do its job, then pull out of the lot with a heavy heart.

If I hadn't already told my mother when I planned on arriving in town, I would look up the nearest motel and be done with it. But the fact is I did tell her, and I don't have it in me to come up with an excuse for why I avoided her. She actually seemed enthused over the phone and immediately demanded I stay with her. *It can be just like old times.*

I have to wonder if she deliberately deludes herself, or if she has truly lost touch with reality. I wouldn't know. The most we ever touch base comes in the form of a brief phone call every two or three weeks. We never go beyond the surface-level small talk. The weather, health, work. There's never anything real. We don't share ourselves.

Soon I'm outside the heart of town, the well-lit streets turn into winding, two-lane roads where lights are planted sporadically, leaving entire patches of road dark and icy in spots. I flip on my high beams and drive carefully, while in the back of my mind I try to figure out exactly when we started drifting apart. Our relationship wasn't exactly healthy even before I left for Boston when I was eighteen and starting college. She might have assumed I was coming home after graduation, since I never told her I was applying to grad school in Virginia.

It was one of those things I wanted to keep quiet until I knew for sure whether or not I was accepted. She took it as an example of me shutting her out of my life. There was no convincing her otherwise and to be honest, I didn't have it in me to keep trying. Once she makes her mind up, that's it. You can't convince her otherwise.

So I gave up, like I gave up trying to nurture a relationship between us. It always seems like we're talking past each other. Sometimes it's like she speaks in code. Like she expects me to unravel her somehow. I don't have the time or the energy or, frankly, the patience. The busier I got with school, the further apart we drifted and the less I was able to visit.

To be honest, I could have tried a little harder, but I can't think of anyone who'd look forward to their entire ugly, terrible past slapping them in the face. The way mine did today.

And it wasn't entirely my fault. I have to remind myself of that so I don't spiral into self-reproach as I draw closer to the house with every turn of the wheels. Mom's taste in men didn't exactly help things. My one-time stepfather was a real piece of work. Loud, brash, lazy. The kind of man who would brag that he never eats a vegetable or reads a book. The opposite of my father, in other words.

Watching him stroll around the house and act like it was his own used to make my blood boil, even if I did my damnedest to hide my feelings. It didn't matter. He didn't like me very much, either. *What is it about you that makes your mother so sad when you come around?*

He actually had the nerve to ask me that question once, like he was accusing me of ruining his good time. When I reminded him of Maddie and how much we look alike— or would, if she were still alive— the conversation took a turn I'll never forget. Before I knew it, we were shouting at each other from opposite sides of the dining room table, with me telling him he'd never replace my father and him reminding me of how my father shot and nearly killed a man on the courthouse steps. How he fell to pieces after Maddie's death. How he did time before being released and moving to a trailer on the outskirts of town. *He's a bum and a loser and he broke your mother's heart. You say I'm not like him? Damn right, I'm not.*

Yet he broke her heart, too. They were never going to last. I knew it the minute I met him, but some things a person has to learn on their own. They were too different. She was too lonely and too willing to open her heart to the first man who came along and promised a sense of security she'd lost a long time ago.

I'm also fairly certain he abused her, no matter how adamantly she denied it.

Not to mention the way he enabled habits she picked up in the wake of Maddie and everything that happened after. I wonder if anyone who's never had a history of addiction in their family understands what it's like to see a loved one's name on their caller ID and immediately feel their heart sink and their defenses rise. I never knew which version of Mom I was going to get if and when I answered.

Would she be bubbly and buzzed and full of hope? Would she be morose, depressed, wallowing in misery? Or maybe she'd be somewhere in between, drunk but not drunk enough that she'd started to spiral yet. After a while, I had to stop engaging with her for the sake of my own sanity. It was only after the divorce from Phil that we started talking again, even as sporadically as we do. It's still better than it was before, but no less stressful. She's still a wild card.

And that's why I can't bring myself to get out of the car once I've cut the engine, sitting in the driveway alongside the house. My God, here I am. The strangest sense of the past and present overlapping sinks into my bones as I sit and stare up at the rambling old Victorian in which I grew up. I see it as it was then and as it is now at the same time.

The navy blue trim has been bleached white, highlighted against the cerulean siding of the house. Soft lamplight from the streetside fixtures glints off the snow-covered roof, and warm rays pour out through the windows of the first floor, stirring a strange ache of longing.

The stained glass window in the attic is still as breathtaking as ever—Mom likes to keep a light on up there in the evening, so everyone who goes past can admire the vibrant, red rose in the center of sapphire blue glass panes. I used to love playing up there when I was little, staring out at the world through that blue and red glass that turned everything from plain and ordinary to colorful and mysterious.

How many hours did I spend on the porch swing, curled up with a book? Maddie used to tease me and call me a bookworm and promised that one day, I would be more interested in going out with my friends and dating boys than I would be in my books. I would only laugh and shake my head and tell her how weird she was. I would never be like her, I swore, even though that's all I wanted to be deep down inside. I just never thought I could compete. She was so pretty, vibrant, popular. The opposite of me, in other words.

That's what's missing from the house now, I realize. Life. Sure, there's lights on inside, and I'm pretty sure I see my mother's shadow pass behind one of the windows. But there's no life in there. It's almost like she's living in and maintaining a mausoleum. A hulking structure filled with memories of what used to be in better times.

And here I am, about to walk into it, hoping I don't get sucked into the endless chasm of grief that's never been processed fully.

I'm still of half a mind to back out and drive as fast as I can, as far away as I can. She's too quick for me. The porch light flips on only a second before the front door opens and my mother appears, shoving her arms through the sleeves of a thick cardigan that almost swallows her thin frame.

It's too late now. *Here goes nothing.*

Chapter 6

I haven't yet unlocked the door before mom is already halfway down the steps, arms wrapped around her middle to keep her sweater closed. "You'll catch your death out here," I call out as I step onto the driveway, and it's not lost on me that I sound just like she always did back when I was little. Catching her death? It's like being back here has turned me into an old lady.

You were born old. Maddie's gentle, playful admonishment echoes in the back of my head like wind chimes in the moment before Mom reaches me. To my surprise, she throws her arms around me and squeezes tight. This is new. We are not very touchy feely anymore.

"Oh, honey. I am so glad to see you." She squeezes tight enough to make me wince, but I can't pretend there isn't something deeply necessary about being wrapped in one of her fierce hugs. The scent of her Ivory soap— she's never stopped using it, always swearing it's the key to her youthful complexion— takes me back and softens my heart and is almost enough to knock me back against the car. It's that powerful.

And here I was, thinking we'd sit and stare at each other, and only if we spent any time together. When Phil was part of her life, I tended to hole up in my room to avoid being in his presence. It sort of became a habit.

"Come on, let's get inside. You must be starved after a long day. I fixed all your favorites." She eyes my single duffel bag when I pull it from the back seat. "You always were a light packer," she murmurs. I'll pretend there's no judgment in that.

"Nobody wants to think a case like this is going to keep them in town for very long." Yes, that sounds like a reasonable excuse.

"Sure, I can understand that. That poor couple." There is a note of wistfulness in her voice, but it's gone in an instant once she opens the front door and ushers me inside. "Welcome home."

Home? "What did you do here?" I set my

bag down, eyes wide. My brain doesn't want to accept what I'm looking at.

"What do you think? I've been dying to see your reaction."

I can barely gather my thoughts before she takes off my coat and hangs it near the front door, then pulls me by the elbow from the front entry hall into the dining room. Like many homes of this style, there's a wide hallway running from the front door straight through to the back, and the stairs stretch along the left-hand side, leading to the second floor. To either side of the hall are the living room on the right and the dining room past that, while to the left there's what Mom used to call the parlor— that was the nice room, the room for company, the room we weren't supposed to hang out in unless we wanted to get yelled at. Beyond that is the room she used as her private space to house supplies for the many passions she's enjoyed over the years.

But it's all so ... different.

"The place needed lightening up, you know?" Her excited energy makes me nervous. Is she buzzed? I take in her appearance, jeans, a long sleeve turtleneck, leopard print flats. It's a lot better than her pajamas and a pair of slippers. Her hair is a lighter shade of brown than mine and it looks like it might be freshly cut, blown out into loose waves she's pulled into a low ponytail. She looks good, better than I've seen her in a long time. I wish I didn't have to feel so suspicious.

Sure, the house needed some lightening up, but the idea used to be to keep it as close to its original appearance as possible. That was the whole point. Mom and Dad wanted to open a bed and breakfast here, hence purchasing the house in the first place. They didn't want to make it look modern and bright and airy.

Now, everything is... white. Very white. Modern farmhouse like on HGTV. Even the gorgeous, carved banister running up the stairs has been painted over. It does make a huge difference, along with the change in furnishings that I notice as she whisks me down the hall. I barely have time to take in the contemporary sitting area in the living room and parlor before we're already in the dining room, where a platter of eggplant parmesan awaits, along with a huge bowl of pasta, a basket of garlic bread, and sauteed greens.

"You really went all out!" It's sweet, and it melts some of the protective ice that's built up around my heart. I can almost let myself hope she's made a positive change that will stick.

"It isn't every day my girl comes home." She practically forces me into a chair. It's brand new, I notice, and a far cry from the heavy, antique dining set that used to live in this room.

"You look tired." She pats my cheek before taking the plate from in front of me and loading it with food. All the while, her mouth moves. "You haven't been getting enough sleep, have you? You can't do your job effectively if you are sleep deprived all the time."

I haven't gotten much sleep because I've been dreading this. Something tells me she won't appreciate that. It's true, though. I hardly slept a wink last night and set out early this morning, wanting to hit the ground running after I arrived. And I did. But I'm starting to feel the effects now, for sure. I guess it's showing up on my face.

Before I can offer an explanation, she's on to the next topic. "Please, tell me you're seeing somebody nice."

"Nice?" My laughter is awkward, uncomfortable.

"I'm just saying, I would like to know if you

found somebody nice. It's been too long since you've spoken of anybody you're dating."

"Because there's nobody worth talking about right now."

I don't think she hears me. "What about the case? I saw the press conference. It cut into my talk show. Those poor people. I remember that hopeless feeling." She pauses for a second while filling her plate, her gaze drifting toward the window.

Then she snaps out of it all at once and smiles. "It's a shame it takes something like this to bring you home, but I'm glad to have you here. So, what do you think of the changes I've made with the house?" She plops into the chair across from mine and I notice the way her hazel eyes sparkle.

"Are you feeling alright?" I take an experimental bite of the eggplant and find it absolutely delicious, well-seasoned and crisp.

"Never better, really." I must look skeptical, since she blows out an exasperated sigh. "You will never get tired of mothering me, will you?"

"I'm sorry. It just seems like a lot all at once."

"Considering you haven't seen the house in

three years, you don't know how sudden all of this is."

She's not wrong. "You've never talked about renovating."

"I didn't know I had to clear it with you first." She turns her attention to her food, muttering under her breath. Already, we're drifting apart and the room feels chillier. This has to be a record.

"I think it looks really nice, don't get me wrong. Really, it's beautiful. It just took me by surprise."

"That was the idea." She looks a little happier as she reaches for a piece of garlic bread. "I've been wanting a new start, and this seemed like as good a starting place as any."

"So you've been feeling good lately?" I make it a point to focus on my food rather than looking her way. I don't want her seeing the hopeful intensity I'm sure is written all over my face.

"If you're asking whether I've been drinking, the answer is no. I've been sober for six months."

"Yeah? That's great. I'm so happy to hear that." Do I believe her? I do. But I'm not going to invest much hope this time around. I learned a long time ago how important it is to protect myself while wanting the best for her.

"I've never felt better." Suddenly she drops her utensils onto the plate. "I almost forgot to show you."

"Show me what?" And I thought she was exhausting when she was drinking? I can't keep up with her now.

She disappears for a minute, then returns holding a business card out for me to have a look. "Eleanor Forrest, Broker." I don't know which part of that to tackle first. The fact that she went back to using Dad's last name after she divorced Phil, or the fact that she got her real estate license back.

"I'm about to close on my first house." She's glowing as she returns to her chair.

"Are you still with Chuck's office? Or are you with another broker now?"

"I worked things out with Chuck. I think having Phil out of the picture helped." She purses her lips and goes silent, and I know that's the end of the topic.

Phil was the kind of guy who always had an excuse for why he couldn't make a steady income, yet he somehow also had a problem with my mother earning money with her off-

and-on real estate work. She ended up letting the license lapse, and things got ugly for a little while. That's around the time she started drinking, come to think of it.

By the time I finish eating, I'm pretty sure my waistband is cutting off my circulation. "I can't remember when I last ate this well. Thank you for going to the trouble."

"Honey, it's no trouble. I'm so happy you're here, I'd spend all day cooking if I had to." When I stand and start to gather dishes, she waves her hands before hopping out of her chair. "Leave that to me. You'll want to get settled in."

Yes, but I'm not looking forward to going upstairs. I'm not sure if I hope my bedroom looks the same as before or if I'll wish that she had made the same kind of changes upstairs as she has down here. I can't go the rest of my life avoiding the past. I know that. But that doesn't mean I can face it now.

"Come on. Let me finish showing you around before I clean this up." I'm still a little off-balance as we walk through the first floor and she explains in detail the changes she's made.

Again, there's that sense of the past and the present overlapping. I still see the dark wallpaper, the heavy drapes, the old fashioned furniture that was actually a lot more comfortable than it looked in most cases. Instead of shelves crammed with books in the living room, they're artfully displayed along with small succulents and little tchotchkes. The old windows have been replaced and the floors now boast shining, restored hardwood.

"There's so much more sunlight and life now," she comments. "I realized it was time to stop waiting for something that would never happen."

The bed and breakfast, I guess. I can't blame her for wanting to move on rather than living in limbo. "It looks fantastic."

"Of course, I haven't had the chance to attack the rooms upstairs yet. I'll have to close on a few houses before I can start thinking along those lines."

That answers my question. Everything will be the same as it was the last time I was here, and the time before that, and five years before then. I don't know how to feel about that, whether it's a good thing or not.

"I have an idea. Why don't you stay in the

guest room instead of your old room? It's so much more comfortable. Less cluttered."

"There's a guest room?"

"Sure. Come and see." Her lips twitch with barely contained humor as she leads me into the hall and past the parlor. "Enough of cramming this room with things I'll never use. This is a much better use of the space."

A guest bedroom. She turned her old She Cave— her term for it— into a guest bedroom with an ensuite bathroom visible through an open door beside the bed.

"This is beautiful." I run my hand over the striped duvet, its delicate blue and white pattern matching the curtains and a throw arranged expertly over the back of an armchair placed near the bay window that faces the garden. There's not much to see out there at this time of year, but it does my heart good when I notice how neat everything looks. No dead overgrowth sticking up through the snow, and the fence around it looks well maintained.

"I'm sure you'll be more comfortable down here. You're a grown woman, not a teenager anymore. Although you know," she adds on her way to the door, "there are some things up there you might want to keep. I haven't touched anything, but eventually I'll want to make some space. If you have time ..."

She trails off on her way to the dining room, where I hear her humming happily as she gathers plates and bowls. I'm not sure who this woman is anymore. I mean, I'm thrilled she seems to be doing so well, but this about-face leaves me feeling a little unsteady. I don't know what to expect.

One thing I know for sure: I am not in any hurry to go upstairs. Maybe it's not the most mature way to handle the situation, but the idea of facing all those memories and having to walk past Maddie's room on my way to and from my own is not something I feel like tackling. I might have to conveniently forget to go up there and clear out some of my old things.

It's not as if there's anything I'm interested in keeping, anyway.

Chapter 7

"Seriously, you do not need to go to all this trouble. How much do you think I eat, anyway?"

My mother only laughs and waves a dismissive hand. "You have no idea how much I wished I could have the time to make breakfasts like this for you when you were a kid."

As I sit down at the kitchen table in front of a plate of French toast and eggs, I can't help snickering when I remember the Pop Tart that used to be my go-to breakfast. She might have gone out for donuts or muffins on a Saturday morning, but even then it was sporadic. For the most part, I was on my own.

"Everything looks delicious." There's plenty

of steaming coffee, too, and a pitcher of orange juice.

She rubs her arms briskly before grabbing her coffee and taking a sip. "Somehow, the cold still manages to get through these new windows."

"And just think, it's not even winter yet."

"Don't remind me. If you find me frozen to death, you'll understand why."

Then why did you stay? There's a question I've asked myself more times than I can count. I've never found the courage to ask her, though. I doubt I ever will. But I know I wasn't the only person in town surprised she decided to keep the house after Dad went away and they split up. She could have sold it and made a mint. I always felt it was sort of like living in a museum full of history— and not the kind of history a person wants to look back on. Now that I've gotten over the surprise of her renovations, I can completely understand why she would go to the trouble. It's good that she wants to start fresh. And it's about time, too.

"So." She takes her time cutting a piece of French toast which she then dips lightly into a small cup of syrup. She never did like dousing her plate, the way I do. No wonder she seems to stay so effortlessly thin. "What's the plan today?"

"I would like to talk with Camille's friends. Her parents gave me their names yesterday."

"You think they might know something?"

"I have to follow every lead. Sometimes it takes a day or two for somebody to remember things they didn't think about when they were first questioned. Especially kids. They might think they're protecting their friend or themselves, depending on what it is they were afraid to share."

"She was a nice girl. One of the good ones." I'm not going to point out the fact that she's using past tense.

I have to bite my tongue or else risk blurting out what instantly came to mind. Maddie was a good girl, too. And look what happened to her. When it comes to terrible situations like this, it doesn't always matter. It's better for us to both focus on eating breakfast— clearly, she feels the same way, since the room falls silent.

Until my phone buzzes. "Excuse me," I murmur, reaching into my pocket to pull it out. The call is coming from the police station,

76

though there's no way of knowing the extension or anything like that. It might be the captain, or it could be some jerk wanting to give me a hard time before I even step foot in the building this morning.

"Agent Forrest? Captain wants you. I'll email you the location."

"What's the matter? Has—" *Has Camille been found?*

"They found a body. He wants you right away. I'll send you the location now." With that, the call ends, leaving me reeling. I can barely find the breath to tell Mom I have to go before I rush out into the front hall for my coat, then head out into a gloomy, drizzly morning. A lot of the snow has already been washed away by the rain that fell overnight, making everything slushy and leaving deep puddles for my tires to splash in. Thank goodness it's not cold enough to freeze over. One or two degrees can make all the difference.

As soon as the Google Maps image comes through, I know where I'm headed. The body— whoever it happens to belong to— was found along the two-mile route between the bookstore and Camille's home.

I spot the white canopy from a distance and head toward it with my heart aching. There's always the chance an investigation is going to turn out like this, after all. But that doesn't make it any easier. Especially now, knowing the parents. There is no easy way to handle this sort of situation. There's no protecting myself when the case is so similar to my sister's.

One thing is immediately clear as I park the car and raise the hood of my coat before stepping out, whoever left the body here left it sometime between yesterday afternoon and now, since there was nothing remotely out of place when I drove this route before. And considering the position of the canopy set up to protect the integrity of the scene, the body is near the side of the road. No way would I have missed that, to say nothing of the search and rescue teams who've already combed the area.

Right away, I spot Andy Cobb's blond hair. Somehow it gleams even on a cloudy, rainy day. He lifts a hand in greeting as I approach. "Body was found near the drainage ditch," he announces before I've had the chance to ask. "Guy got a flat tire early this morning and pulled over, waiting for a tow. I swear, it's like nobody knows how to change a flat tire anymore. I guess handling things on your own is a lost art."

I can't tell if he's trying to annoy me or just the type who has an opinion on everything.

"If he knew how to fix his own tire, he might not have noticed the body."

He leads me toward the scene, then drinks from a steaming cup of coffee while I take it all in. I pull a pair of latex gloves from my pocket — I make it a point to carry a spare wherever I go, just in case. "She matched the description?" I ask while carefully picking my way down a steep embankment, muddy and slushy and dangerous.

"Young girl, fair skin, long, dark hair."

It's a battle between maintaining profession-alism and mourning for the Martins as I finish my descent, then carefully lift the plastic tarp placed over the body.

"It's not her." All the air in my lungs rushes out in one long breath. "The bone structure is all wrong. And she has a small mole on her chin — Camille doesn't."

"The Martins will be relieved," Andy muses from his spot further up the embankment.

"I'm sure they will." I stand up straight, shaking my head as I stare down at the dead girl. "Until it hits them there's somebody out here, killing teenagers."

And we're still no closer to finding Camille. Has she already met this girl's fate? Or is there still time?

Chapter 8

I check my notes one more time while sitting in the visitors lot. Lila Kirkman was fourteen years old and originally from an old family who've lived on the Main Line outside Philadelphia for generations. She has family in the area, and that's probably why they considered sending her to a boarding school in Maine. Hawthorne is considered one of the top schools in New England, so I'm sure that must have influenced their decision, as well. According to the captain, they've been informed and are on their way.

Every parent's worst nightmare. How many times have I heard that in the last twenty years? So many that the phrase has lost all meaning. I know very well what every parent's worst nightmare is. I lived through it. I watched my parents' marriage crumble like stale bread. Situations like this either bring people closer or drive a wedge between them.

I wonder what it will do to Lila's parents.

Now that we have a confirmed identification thanks to dental records, it's time to start asking questions around the school. *The Academy.* That's how regulars refer to it, whereas Broken Hill High is *The School.*

Because, God forbid, anybody ever confuse the two.

Sitting in the heart of campus, it's pretty clear there is no confusing them. My old high school is an impressive building surrounded by grounds that are cared for and maintained well. Hawthorne Academy, on the other hand, has an entire campus that brings to mind Harvard or some other fancy Ivy League school. I might not have gone there, but I'm familiar with the campus, and the stately buildings with wide, rolling lawns bring it to mind. There is not so much as a trace of slush on the pathways criscrossing each other, pathways students now travel on foot as they make their way to their next class.

Forest of Silence

The dorms sit on opposite sides of campus. One for the girls, one for the boys. I walk to the girls' dorm, and I can't help but admire how pristine everything is. There's not so much as a scrap of litter on the ground. Not a cigarette butt, an empty can of energy drink, nothing. I'm sure it's stunning in spring, once the trees get their leaves and the grass turns emerald green.

"I told him I would think about it," a girl explains to a friend as they pass, both of them wearing the pleated navy skirt and knee-high socks that are part of the school uniform. "But honestly, I don't know how I'll have the time to volunteer when I'm already living on four hours of sleep at night."

"But it will look great on your transcripts," her friend points out. "Score that internship in Portland this summer and you're golden." I'm not sure if I'm listening to a pair of teenagers or middle-aged business women. It really is like another world here.

The girls' dorm used to be the home of one of Broken Hill's founding members. McNulty Hall is named for the man who built it to house his family— if I remember correctly, they had twelve kids, not to mention a full staff. I guess he figured he needed a small castle, which is the first word that comes to mind as I approach the sprawling, grey stone structure.

When I reach out to open one of the double doors, I grunt in frustration to find it locked. They have to have some sort of security system in place around here, I guess. Until now, nobody has given me so much as a second glance as I walked across campus. They can't make it that easy for predators to stroll into a dorm.

"Can I help you?" The disembodied voice comes from somewhere over my head, and when I look up I find a camera mounted discreetly above the doors. There's a speaker to my right, along with an electronic keypad.

"I'm FBI agent Alexis Forrest." I hold up my badge so it can be plainly seen in the camera. "I'm working with the local authorities and I'm here to ask some questions about one of the girls who resides in this building."

The keypad buzzes before I can say another word, and soon I'm inside an entry hall so grand it takes my breath away. I also feel very small—the ceiling is a good thirty feet over my head, and from it hangs a heavy, iron chandelier. Mr. McNulty didn't believe in playing small, obviously. It reminds me of one of those old estates in Europe, the kind you see in historical dramas. Heavy wooden beams span the ceiling, while the wood paneled walls feature paintings of what I assume is the McNulty family, along with images from Broken Hill's past.

I'm starting to wonder how I'm supposed to find the person I need to talk to when a stunning older woman wearing a beautifully fitted suit strides my way. Her heels click smartly against the floor, and she lowers the glasses perched on top of her head before extending a hand to shake. "Agent Forrest. I'm Adele Johnson, Dean of Girls. We just got word from the police. To say I'm heartbroken would be a tremendous understatement." Now I understand why she had removed her glasses. Up close, it's clear to see she's been crying, her eyes red and watery despite her friendly expression.

"I'm very sorry for your loss. I was hoping to speak to Lila's resident advisor and roommates, if possible."

"Of course. Anything we can do to help. Poor Lila." She gestures for me to follow her, and I almost have to jog to keep up with her quick gait. "Would you like some coffee or tea? A bottle of water?"

"No, thank you."

"I'll have the girls called in to meet with you in my office." We step into what was probably considered the family library back in the day, a room that features a wide, tall fireplace of gleaming white marble. The fire blazing cheerfully inside makes the cavernous space seem warm and cozy.

"Please come and have a seat," she urges, and I choose a high-backed leather chair positioned in front of the fire. It's so warm I have to take my coat off, and I'm glad to have a chance to shake the chill that's settled into my bones.

Once the dean makes a phone call requesting the girls be sent down, I ask, "Is there anything you can tell me, Dean Johnson? Did you know Lila personally?"

"We crossed paths every day," she says. Sorrow hangs heavy in her voice as she rounds what looks like an antique desk positioned in front of frosted windows. "This is only her first year, you understand, but I found her to be warm and bubbly. Very sweet. And there was never so much as a whisper of trouble. Her mother and father are both Hawthorne alumni. She understood the importance of tradition and wanted to make her parents proud."

Another good girl. I'm starting to see a pattern. I don't have the time to ask more questions, because a bleary-eyed girl sort of wanders into the room, blowing her nose before shoving the tissue into her pocket. She's not wearing her uniform, I notice, but rather a set of flannel pajama pants and an oversized hoodie.

"As soon as I heard, I lost it," she whispers to the dean, who rubs her back and murmurs in understanding.

"Agent Forrest, this is Veronica Carson."

Veronica sits across from me, arms folded over her midsection. "I am— was— Lila's RA. I was up all night hoping she would show up. Like it was all a misunderstanding or something."

"What can you tell me?" I ask in a soft voice. This girl is devastated. I need to be gentle. "I understand she went missing last night."

Her head bobs up and down while she gulps. "She went for dinner at the cafeteria with her roommates, and they had plans to see a movie that's playing down at the student center. Lila didn't feel like going, so she told them she'd see them in the dorm when they came back. Only when they got here, she wasn't in her room. They couldn't get a hold of her, either."

"And that's unlike her?"

"Super unlike her. She was supposed to be working on a project, and she always took that kind of thing seriously. And if she were ever going to be late, she would check in with one of the girls to let them know so nobody would worry. So when it was ten o'clock and they still couldn't find her, they let me know, and we went down to campus security."

Yes, that's who our report came from. Apparently, they searched for a few hours before calling the station around one in the morning to report her missing.

Her body was found at six. Whoever did this wasn't wasting any time. Right away, I'm struck by the contrast with Camille's case. Then again, who's to say her body isn't out there somewhere and we simply haven't discovered it yet?

Lila's roommates aren't in much better shape than their RA. Christie and Dakota are both weeping when they enter the dean's office. Adele hugs them both and murmurs her condolences before they sit close together on the leather sofa facing the fire.

"Of course, we don't expect the girls to attend class at a time like this," Adele explains before turning to the girls. "And I've contacted the grief counselor. She's available whenever you want to talk. I strongly urge you to visit her today." I get the feeling she's extremely devoted to the girls, which I guess makes it even harder to deal with something like this. You can be just as devoted as the day is long, but the worst can happen anyway.

"I only have a few questions," I tell them as gently as I can. A quick glance toward the dean conveys my message and she makes herself scarce, giving me the chance to talk to the girls without an authority figure looming over us.

"I can't believe it," Dakota mumbles, leaning against her friend. "She said she was coming back to work on her project. We should've gone with her. We shouldn't have gone to the movie."

"Nothing that happened is your fault." At least, as far as I know. "You couldn't have known this would happen. Don't blame yourselves."

"Do you think she was scared?" Christie's eyes are wide, haunted. She's fourteen, but she might as well be a toddler asking for reassurance when the monsters under the bed seem too real.

"I really don't know," I murmur. "Right now, we need to work on finding who did this. There will be plenty of time for those questions later." I should know.

I clear my throat, looking down at my notepad, my pen poised. "Did Lila have friends outside of school? Off campus, I mean? Somebody she might have been going to see after dinner?"

The girls exchange a look. They don't have to say a word. The hair on the back of my neck lifts but I manage to keep myself even keel so they will stay calm. "Can you tell me who it is?"

"There was a boy." Dakota rocks slightly like she's comforting herself. "But there weren't any issues."

"They were only dating for a little while," Christie explains. "Not even two months yet."

"What's his name? Do you know where I can find him? Did she tell you anything about him?"

"He plays hockey, and he's really good at it. He's in eleventh grade at Broken Hill High."

A junior dating a freshman? Interesting. But not necessarily a red flag just yet. "Can you tell me his name?"

"Danny," Dakota murmurs before wiping a tear from her cheek. "Danny Clifton. She never stopped talking about him."

Danny Clifton.

Why does that name ring a bell? I flip a few

pages back to the notes I took yesterday, and right away the name jumps out at me. I stalked his social media last night.

Danny Clifton was the boy Camille dated last year.

Chapter 9

Visiting Beacon Hill High immediately after touring the grounds of Hawthorne only highlights the stark difference between the two schools. I see everything through a different lens as I climb out of my Corolla and take a deep breath of the damp air. It hasn't stopped drizzling all day, and what was once snow covered has become bleak and depressing thanks to the muddy bits of slush still clinging to life in ugly patches on grass that's browned and dead. The world exists in washed-out shades of gray and brown, and a light wind is enough to drive the dampness into my bones.

This the sort of day when a cup of hot chocolate and a bowl of steaming soup would come in handy. Instead, I walk briskly with my chin tucked close to my chest, the hood of my coat catching the worst of the wind driven raindrops before they hit my face, soaking into my hair. I could use a hot bath and might treat myself to one once I call it a day, but that's not going to happen for a while. I know better than to think otherwise.

"You're here to see Clifton?" The school's hockey coach looks understandably skeptical, eyeing me warily at the entrance to the rink that sits in a building separated from the school by the football field and the track that runs around it. A couple dozen high school boys are out there in the middle of practice, while a handful of students— girls, for the most part— are scattered around in the bleachers.

"Yes, sir. I have a few questions to ask him." I make it a point to show my badge, which only intensifies his narrow-eyed stare. "I won't keep him for long, I promise. I understand you're looking at a winning season here. I don't want to get in the way of that."

"Yeah, and Danny is the standout." I feel the heavy implication behind his words, and the slight edge of ... what is it? It's almost like he's accusing me of something, though I haven't spoken to the kid yet. I haven't even told him why I'm here, though if Danny has already been questioned as one of Camille's contacts, word has probably spread. I'm sure he can assume.

"Like I said. I only have a few questions. He'll be back on the ice in no time." As a last-ditch effort, I add, "I wish our hockey team had done so well back when I was here. I'm pretty sure those guys barely knew how to skate before they joined the team."

He can't fight back a tiny grin. "Yeah, we started turning things around a couple seasons back. Danny's going to take us to the championship." With that, he looks across the ice and lifts a hand. "Clifton! Somebody wants to talk to you." He shows me to the players' box, where I take a seat on the bench and observe the effect Danny has on the kids sitting above me as he approaches.

There is nothing in the world that quite matches the sound of a girl with a crush. From the stifled giggles and breathless whispers, something tells me there is a lot of interest going around, and they're all directed at the tall, dark-haired boy with the killer smile. He directs that smile over my head when one of the girls calls his name. They'd better be careful or they're going to start to swoon.

I was a teenage girl once. I remember how it felt when I would see Mitch coming my way. We could be in a hallway choked with people, bodies moving in all directions, but somehow there was a spotlight focused squarely on him. Everything around him went sort of hazy, cloudy. My stomach would flutter and my knees would go weak. I lived for those moments. Every time I turned a corner, I hoped to find him waiting. There was never any telling when he would show his face and make my day worthwhile. That's the power a cute boy has over a teenage girl.

I feel their gaze lingering on me as I extend a hand to the school's hockey star. "Danny. My name is Agent Forrest."

He sets his helmet down beside him, and his smile is nowhere to be seen when he turns my way. "I already told the cops everything I know."

So that's how it's going to be. Fine with me. Note to self, subject is surly. "I understand that, but I'm not a cop. I'm an FBI agent. I came to town to investigate Camille Martin's disappearance, and now—"

"Lila."

"Right." He seems pretty matter of fact,

considering she's dead and they were supposedly dating. Don't jump to conclusions. Sometimes it's difficult not to, especially when a guy whose girlfriend couldn't stop talking about him seems fairly unaffected by her tragic loss. Did he ever shine that killer smile her way?

"What can you tell me about her? I understand from speaking with her roommates that the two of you dated for a little while."

"Yeah."

"That's pretty interesting. A boy from Broken Hill High and a girl from Hawthorne Academy. I'm a Broken Hill girl," I explain before he has the chance to ask what I know about it. "Back in my day, the Hawthorne kids couldn't be bothered to hang out with us, much less date one of us."

"Yeah, it's not that much different now."

"But somehow you two found each other."

"Some people aren't snobs. Lila came to a dance here at school. The girl she came with is hanging out with a guy from the team, and we ended up talking. You know, the sort of stuff you talk about when you first meet somebody and you don't think you're going to have a lot in common with them."

"But you did have enough in common?"

Forest of Silence

"Sure." He chuckles, running a hand over his slightly sweaty hair. "I mean, it's like you said. I figured girls from Hawthorne wouldn't be caught dead with a guy from here. But she was cool. Like, normal. We could just talk like two people. It didn't feel like I had to, I don't know, apologize for not being rich."

"Yeah, I remember how that felt. I guess not much has changed."

"When did you graduate?"

"It was twelve years this past June."

"In Broken Hill, things sort of stand still, don't they?" His almost sheepish grin could make anyone at school fall for him. When a couple of girls whimper— at least, that's how it sounds— his gaze darts in their direction. He heard them. And the way the corners of his mouth twitch tells me he likes the attention. I have to force myself not to jump to conclusions, but the profile coming together in my mind doesn't leave much room for the benefit of the doubt. He's terribly aware of the effect he has on his classmates. There's being handsome and popular, and then there's knowing exactly how handsome and popular you are.

"What did your friends think when they

97

found out you were dating a girl from Hawthorne?"

He shrugs good naturedly. "I don't know. What did I think when I found out they were dating girls from our school? It doesn't really matter." Then, he snickers in a quiet way. "It probably matters more to the Hawthorne kids. Like they're slumming it."

"But not Lila?"

"No way. As soon as she told me she plays Civ, I knew she was cool."

"Civ? What's that?"

The look that comes over his face is almost sympathetic. Like he feels sorry for me. "Civilization. You've never heard of it?"

"I don't think so. What is it?"

I can't remember the last time I saw somebody's eyes light up the way his did. "It's a computer game. It's been around for years, since way back in the day. There've been six versions of it so far— they're supposed to be working on a seventh, but it's only speculation right now. When I asked her what she does for fun, that was the first thing she said …"

His gaze softens, as does the curve of his mouth. "It was pretty cool. I have never met a

Forest of Silence

girl who plays computer games, especially not my favorite game."

Now that he's feeling bright and engaged, I want to keep him this way. "So, what do you do? Shoot people?"

"No, it's not like that. It's almost like a board game, but you play it on the computer. We'd sometimes play with each other remotely. You choose the leader you want to play as— all kinds of historical figures, like Cleopatra and Teddy Roosevelt, from all different countries and eras. And then, you start building cities, you meet other civilizations, you go to war with them."

"That sounds really interesting. I never liked violent games."

"I mean, even the wars aren't really violent." He blurts out a sheepish laugh. "I've got, like, two thousand hours in the game so far. Don't tell my coach. He thinks I'm working out and stuff."

We both glance toward the man in question, who's trying and not doing a very good job of making it look like he isn't trying to get a feel for our conversation. "Your secret is safe with me."

"So you're not going to tell anybody what a nerd I am?"

"You consider yourself a nerd?"

"Some people would."

"But not Lila."

"No, because we could be nerds together."

"When did you find out she went missing?"

His face falls, and all the youthful ease and confidence drains away. His shoulders slump, he leans forward with his forearms braced on his thighs. "I was blowing up her phone all night last night, since she was supposed to call me at eight."

"And it was unusual for you to not hear from her?"

"Did you ever meet the kind of person who schedules everything in their planner? Like, I mean showers, eating, everything? That's Lila. Total Type A. She even scheduled the time she'd play Civ. So yeah, that's unusual."

"But how did you find out she was actually missing and not just, you know, busy?"

"I called around and finally got the number of one of her roommates. Christie. She said ..."

He clears his throat, staring down at his hands. His fingers move, picking at the beds of his thumbnails. Nerves? Anxiety? I hold myself very still, observing every move, every change in his breaths. Breathing that has a slightly strangled quality before he murmurs, "She said Lila never made it back to the dorm. Or if she did, she left again."

"And where were you at the time?"

"I wouldn't hurt Lila."

An interesting thing to say out of the blue. "I didn't say you did. I'm only asking where you were. You said you kept trying to call her."

"I was home. Ask my parents."

Considering the girl is now with the medical examiner, I just might do that.

He blows out a sharp breath and lowers his brow. The way he sticks out his jaw tells me he's feeling bitter. "I know what you're thinking."

"Do you?"

"You think it's too big of a coincidence. Camille and Lila. Right? I already told the cops everything I know about Camille." He bends forward, covering his face with his hands while groaning. "This is like a nightmare. I wish somebody would wake me up."

I won't bother reminding him there are people suffering much worse than he is. "Now that you mention it, why don't we talk about Camille?"

An invisible wall falls between us and he squares his shoulders before standing. "I better get back to practice."

"Your coach can do without you for another few minutes, Danny." I lower my voice, speaking slowly and carefully. "We could always have this conversation at the station, if you'd rather."

I know I've won before he drops back to the bench.

Chapter 10

It's striking, the way his demeanor changes. He sits up straighter than before, rolling his shoulders back while lowering his brow. I wonder if he thinks that's going to intimidate me. "There's nothing to say. I'm bummed she's missing, I really am. I don't know what else to tell you."

"Where were you at the time of Camille's disappearance?"

"The cops already know this."

"I'm not a cop," I remind him. "I'm from the FBI."

"What, they don't tell you these things? You have to do all the work all over again?" He scoffs openly and arches an eyebrow. The sheepish, *aw shucks* nerd is long gone. "How do you get any work done?"

His arrogant attitude might get him far on the ice, but so far all it's managing to do is set my teeth on edge. At times like this, it's a matter of who can wait out the other person. One of us is going to crack, and it's not going to be me. That much I know for sure.

"Indulge me," I murmur, keenly aware of the attention we're still attracting from the kids watching. I have half a mind to ask them to move elsewhere, but that would only stir up more attention.

"I was in Bangor." His smile is snide. "For a game. Plenty of witnesses."

As if I didn't already know. "Danny, let me explain something to you. I'm not asking you questions because I think you're a suspect. I'm asking because I need to know more about Camille. She needs us."

His gaze moves over my face almost like he's trying to decide whether I mean it or not. The slight loosening of his jaw tells me I've passed a test I didn't know I was taking. "Sorry. I guess I watch too much TV. Everybody always questions the ex-boyfriend and assumes there was trouble. But there wasn't. That's what I'm trying to say. Everything was fine ... until it wasn't."

Ever since I was little, I've had what my

father used to jokingly refer to as an inner lie detector. There's never any fooling you, is there? And he was right. I would sometimes wonder why it was so hard for other people to see through lies or half-truths. I used to study body language and facial expressions to the point where Mom would get so unnerved, she would tell me to go play— even if she had only just asked me to help her with something around the house. She couldn't get away with even the sort of simple, innocent lies parents tell their kids. Santa, the tooth fairy, things like that. I was always skeptical.

Looking back, I might have unknowingly robbed myself of some of the so-called childhood magic other kids got to experience. I couldn't help it. It was born in me.

Now, when there's a prickling along the back of my neck, I have to force myself to stay calm. He's finally being real. Maybe he's forgotten we have an audience, too distracted by talk of missing girls who happened to have him in common. "What went down?"

His brow creases and his hands curl into fists. I make note of it on my pad, scrawling the word *fist* without looking. I'm too busy studying him to look away. "I don't know. I never did figure it out. Like, I used to sit around and obsess over it. My friends ... They would never stop making fun of me if they knew, but it really messed with my head. I thought everything was great. I thought we were happy together."

"But she had other ideas."

"Yeah. I didn't know until it was too late."

"What did she say?"

He snorts, staring across the ice where his teammates skate back and forth while the coach blows his whistle until my ears ring. "She said I was too immature."

Those were her exact words?"

"Yep. She needed somebody more adult."

Interesting. From what he's told me, he seems like a fairly levelheaded kid. He must work hard to stay on top of his game. And if Lila— Miss Responsibility, at least from everything I've heard—thought he was worth seeing, there must be something about him Camille overlooked.

"It sounds like she really upset you."

He rolls his eyes and scoffs. "Not enough to, like, kidnap her." He shakes his head. "Even if you're not a cop, you act like one."

I'll overlook that for the sake of our discussion. "How long did you two date?"

"Five months." He rattles the number off without thinking about it, I notice. "She started to, like, pull away. She'd come up with excuses for why she couldn't talk on the phone, why we couldn't hang out. She would tell me she was busy, but it all felt like excuses. I never figured out what I did wrong."

He slides me a look and grimaces. "It took me a little while to get over it."

"I'm sorry to hear that."

"Yeah, well, if she hadn't broken up with me, I wouldn't have met Lila." He turns to me, searching my face again, but there's a different sort of intensity to it this time. "What do you think could have happened? Please, if you know anything, tell me. I barely got any sleep last night, and I'm actually glad you pulled me out of practice because I can't get my head into it today."

Understanding tears through me like a bolt of lightning, tracing a fiery path through my system. "You're worried about Lila?"

His head snaps back while a look of confusion washes over his face. "Yeah, obviously. What, just because I'm in high school, I'm not supposed to care when my girlfriend goes missing?

Oh, no.

Nobody told him yet.

I made an assumption. I thought I was beyond this point, but clearly I have work to do. "Danny ..."

Well, this could turn out to be a lucky accident. I have the chance to get his immediate reaction to the news. The way he reacts will tell me what I need to know about his involvement.

I have to be careful. I wish we were anywhere but here, with so many others around. "Danny, I'm sorry to tell you this. I assumed word had already gotten around to you from one of the girls."

He leans in, his eyes widening. "What? What happened? Where is she? Did you find her?"

Now I sincerely wish we didn't have an audience, for both our sakes. Maybe I should take him somewhere else, to the locker room, or outside. I open my mouth to suggest that, but he shakes his head. "Tell me." The quiet desperation in his voice is clear.

"I'm sorry, Danny. Lila's body was found this morning."

All at once, the color leaves his face. His mouth falls open, his eyes darting this way and that while his brain attempts to make sense of

Forest of Silence

what he just heard. "No. No, there's gotta be a mistake. It can't be Lila. Not Lila."

Reaching out, I cover one of the hands lying limp in his lap. Maybe I shouldn't, but something in me won't let me sit and watch him suffer without offering comfort. "We got confirmation. I'm sorry, but Lila is gone."

He's not the cocky, talented hockey player now. He's a young man who just received a shock. Either that, or he's the most gifted actor ever born. His eyes fill with tears while his mouth moves in one silent protest after another.

Finally our eyes meet and he releases a broken sob before falling against me, his face pressed to my shoulder. "Lila!" It's the only intelligible thing he gets out between wracking sobs.

By now, the team has noticed, and I watch over the top of his head as all activity comes to a stop. The murmuring and whispering behind us falls silent—either that, or Danny's grief is loud enough to drown it out. Grief that echoes in the large, open space. Grief too intense and profound to be an act.

"I'm very sorry for your loss." There's nothing I can do but pat his back while he sobs openly, his tears soaking into my coat, the force of his grief leaving him limp.

This is not an act. I've seen people pretend to be surprised or grieved in a situation like this. Both in person, and in videos during training. Normally, it's easy to spot someone who's over-acting. I've seen suspects pretend to faint, I've seen them throw fits and attempt to tear a room apart, like their rage can't be contained.

I have also seen grieved loved ones fall to pieces. Personally. I've been one of them myself.

And the sort of soul shaking grief currently consuming Danny Clifton is not something that can be faked. It's real. The kid just lost someone he cared about.

All I can do is offer condolences that won't really make a difference in the end. I know that from personal experience, too.

Chapter 11

The first breath of fresh air I pull into my lungs on exiting the rink is a welcome one. It helps clear my head a little, it brings the world into sharper focus. When I exhale, a cloud of vapor expands before me. It's full dark, and the sky has cleared so stars can twinkle above. Stars that could very well be shining down on Camille Martin's corpse while I walk slowly to my car.

My feet are heavy, but not as heavy as my heart. I walked in there hoping to get a feel for the sort of person Danny is. The fact that he dated both girls isn't the sort of connection we can afford to ignore, even if we already knew he was out of town when Camille went missing. But I assumed he'd heard about Lila. I can't make that kind of mistake again, even if it gave me the chance to get his honest reaction.

An honest reaction that's left me shaking and drained by the time I settle in behind the wheel and wait for the heater to work its magic. That poor kid. He really cared for her.

My head weighs roughly a million pounds. I let it rest against the seat back while taking a few deep breaths, though that does nothing for the questions running at full speed through my over-whelmed brain. They were both the kind of girls any parent would be proud of. The sort of girls I would have liked to call my friends when I was their age. Not the kind to run off with a stranger they met online—at least, not according to what I've learned so far. They were both sensible. Goal oriented. And according to Danny, Camille wanted maturity in her life. She doesn't seem like the kind of girl who would take a risk.

Sometimes, there is no deeper answer in cases like this. Sometimes, it's simply a matter of a man or a woman who hunts for easy prey. Sometimes, it's as simple as that. And as endlessly frustrating.

When my phone rings, I wonder if I have it

Forest of Silence

in me to answer. I'm not only physically exhausted. My emotions are wrecked.

But I'm an adult, and I'm here for a job, and I can't afford to pretend I have the option of running away. I'm rewarded, as it turns out, since the call isn't coming from the police station or even from Mom. I put his number in my contacts in case I needed to get in touch with him.

As it turns out, Mitch found a way to get in touch with me.

There's a smile in my voice when I answer, and it's genuine. Considering how low I felt only moments ago, it feels like a small miracle. "I'm supposed to be an FBI agent. How did you manage to get your hands on my number?"

He chuckles, a sound as familiar to me as the sound of my own voice. "I still had your old home number, and your mother hasn't gotten rid of her landline."

Of course, I'm sure a call from Mitch asking for my cell thrilled her to pieces. She never did understand why I broke up with him. Looking back, neither do I, though I had my reasons at the time. I might even have thought they were good reasons.

"Very sneaky." But I'm still smiling, something I didn't think I was capable of tonight. "What can I do for you?"

"I have something here at the shop that I'd like to show you." I barely have time to register the possible double entendre before he laughs. "It's nothing dirty, I promise."

And now I'm disappointed. No, the last thing I need to do is flirt with him. This is not the time or the place for me to indulge my personal needs. "It just so happens I'm in the car and can be with you in ten minutes."

"I'll be here." Is it my imagination, or is my heart beating a little faster than it was before?

I have to remind myself we aren't the kids we used to be, even if it feels that way as I leave the lot and begin the drive into town. Being around the high school has a lot to do with it, I'm sure. The memories are so thick, so plentiful. Everywhere I look, I can't help but think of the way things used to be. I had lost Maddie, sure, along with my father. Living my life meant bearing the scrutiny and the sympathy of countless people, day after day.

But I had Mitch. When we were together, I didn't have to be on guard. There was no reason to feel like I had to hold my breath and wait for an inevitable moment of discomfort to pass. He never got that look on his face like he was remembering Dad being in prison and how he got there. Mitch didn't pity me.

No wonder Mom couldn't figure out why I broke up with him. Right now, I struggle as well. But it's easy to look back more than a decade later and ask questions like that. I'm looking at this situation through the eyes of a thirty-year-old who's seen what else is out there in the world in terms of eligible men and understands what I passed up on. I'm sure it was the right choice in the end. I'm way too involved in my career to make anybody a good girlfriend or wife. At least, that was how Chris always made me feel before we finally ended it a year ago. Mitch deserves better than that.

Does my heart skip a beat when I enter his store, just the same? It sure does. He's standing behind the counter and his head snaps up when the bell chimes. Today, he's wearing a chunky cable knit sweater that leaves me fighting the impulse to rest my head against his chest. He looks so cozy and comforting, and I'm in need of all of that.

And then he does it. He gives me the exact smile I remembered earlier, when I was thinking back to spotting him in the hall during school. It still has the power to knock the wind out of my lungs and make my knees weak.

"Hey. Thanks for coming over."

"How could I resist the invitation when you went to all that trouble to find out how to call me?"

"Yeah, well, you know me. When it comes to you, there's no such thing as too much effort."

He needs to stop saying things like that, or else I might forget why I'm here in the first place. "I can see you're still charming."

"And I can see you still work too hard." He points to the spot between his eyebrows, over the bridge of his nose. "You get these lines here."

"It's been a long day."

"And here I am, keeping you out even later. Maybe I should have waited until tomorrow."

"I'm never too tired for you." Maybe I shouldn't have said that. I mean, it's true, but the way his gaze softens and his smile widens sets off all kinds of fluttery feelings I can't indulge right now. Maybe not ever. Mitch's life is here. Mine isn't.

He does me the favor of clearing his throat first and standing up a little straighter. "I've been thinking. It seems like that's all I can do

is think about anything I might have missed."
He crooks his finger and sets off for the back
of the store. "And I've been looking through
security footage to see if I missed anybody
who might have been following Camille
around."

I need to stop checking out his butt in the
jeans he's wearing. "Have you found
something?"

"I may have. I wanted to bring you in to
take a look." We come to a stop in a small, cluttered office tucked away in the back corner of
the store. There's a laptop open on the desk,
surrounded by folders and boxes of invoices.

"I see you haven't changed."

He glances up from the computer and
smirks. "I'm still a disaster. You can say it."

"You can't be too much of a disaster if
you're running this place."

"Yeah, I've managed to keep the lights on so
far." He steps back, gesturing toward the screen.
"Hit play. You'll see what I mean."

The footage is from a camera behind the
cafe counter. Camille stands at the register— I
can see the top of her head and part of her
profile when she turns to the side. In front of
her stands a man in a polo shirt and slacks who

seems intent on engaging her in conversation. "No sound," Mitch murmurs, apologetic.

"Do you know this guy?" I can't make out too much of his face, unfortunately. Either he deliberately stood where the camera would only pick up part of his sharp profile, or it's simply a matter of bad luck.

"He used to come around every so often," Mitch explains. I need to be careful, or the spicy musk of his cologne will unravel every last stitch of my professionalism. "The kind of guy who would browse around, maybe pick up a book. Sometimes he would only come in for coffee. But when I hired Camille, he was here a few times a week."

"Let me guess. When she was working?"

"You've got it. I didn't think too much about it, honestly— I have a lot on my plate around here."

"You have to stop blaming yourself." Our eyes meet, and in his I find the guilt I knew would be there. "You can't be everywhere at all times. And there are plenty of slightly creepy guys who end up being harmless."

"Thanks, but it doesn't make me feel much better." I didn't think it would, no matter how much I hoped. He's always been too hard on himself. Something we've always had in common. "I can send you some screenshots, if you want."

"For sure. I'll look into it. If you find any other footage of him, send it over as well. I wouldn't mind getting a better look at his face."

"I'll know him when I see him. The next time he shows up around here, I'll pay closer attention."

I won't say it, but if this man is behind Camille's disappearance, he might not come back at all. "Yes, please keep your eye out for me."

"I'm keeping my eye out for her." There's a quiet intensity in his voice that does very unfair things to my heart. There I was, thinking I was over him years ago. It seems I might not have gotten him entirely out of my system.

"Hey," he blurts out while I'm leaving his office. "I'll be closing up in a few. Do you want something to eat?"

On one hand, I should go back to the house. Regroup. Unwind.

On the other hand, I didn't know until now that I was looking for an excuse to spend a little more time here. "Sure. I'm starving. I've been driving around town all day and sort of forgot to eat."

I doubt Mom will mind if I stay out a little longer. Who am I kidding? She's probably kneeling in front of a lit candle, praying that Mitch and I get together.

Chapter 12

There's something about being with Mitch in the otherwise quiet, closed store that has me feeling like I should whisper. Like we're in church. It's incredibly silly, but I can't shake the feeling. I also can't shake the need to watch his every move. This has nothing to do with weighing his reactions, though, the way I did with Danny earlier. I am not interested in Mitch as a suspect, or a possible lead or anything at all related to a case. How refreshing.

No, there's something far different at work. Something stirred up by the time I spent thinking about him earlier. It was one thing seeing him again and being thrust straight back to the old days. It's another to remember how much he meant to me – how much we meant to each other. There were days when he was the only thing that got me out of bed. Knowing I'd be able to see him at school got me moving. I would tell him now if I could find the words. And if I could trust myself not to get emotional while I did. He didn't invite me to spend time with him so I could blubber all over the place.

But maybe one day, I'll let him know. And I'll tell him how grateful I am.

"What are you thinking about right now?"

I almost choke on the tea he insisted I drink when I find him watching me from behind the counter, where he just finished whatever he was doing to close up. "Do you really want to know?"

"I wouldn't have asked, would I? You had a funny look on your face."

I was thinking about you, and how hard it is for me to remember why it was so important that we break up. Right. Because I'm sure that's what he wants to hear. There's no way it wouldn't come off cheesy, not to mention convenient. Anybody can say something like that years after the fact. It doesn't change anything.

I turn the paper cup in my hand, shrugging. "I guess I have a lot on my mind."

"I honestly don't know how you do it." He

straightens out a row of mystery novels before sauntering my way. His gaze sweeps over everything around him like he's looking for anything else that needs to be picked up or put to right before he can officially be done for the day.

"Really, I was thinking more about school. I haven't stepped foot in there since graduation, now I've been on campus twice in the past two days. It's a lot."

"I guess it would be after all these years. Me, I see it all the time. I've learned to live alongside the memories."

He always had an interesting way of expressing himself. I think that was one of the things that attracted me to him the most. His way with words. There was none of the false bravado teenage boys tend to put on when they're trying to look big and impressive. It was enough for him to be himself.

There is so much for us to catch up on. How do I start off? *So, what's life been like for you the past twelve years?* Right. That wouldn't be pitifully awkward at all. "What brought you back here?"

"To Broken Hill?" My head bobs up and down while he jams his hands into his pockets and wanders behind the counter between the table I'm seated at and the coffee machine. "You mean, why didn't I go straight to grad school like you did?"

"You always said you wanted to teach philosophy one day."

The dimple flashes in his cheek when he offers one of his trademark lopsided grins. It still has the power to knock the wind from my lungs. "You remembered."

I will always remember you. "So what happened?"

"Life." He pulls a cloth from under the counter and wipes the Formica surface, though it already looked pretty clean from where I'm sitting. "Mom got sick."

"Oh, no. I had no idea." And how many times did my mother fill me in on the mundane gossip about people I couldn't have cared less about? But this, she kept from me.

"Breast cancer," he continues. "But she made a full recovery. She's been healthy as a horse for seven years now."

"I am so glad. Tell her I said hi, would you?"

"Sure thing."

Seven years. That's still plenty of time for him to get his life back on track. I would never come out and say it that way, though I'm curious. "What led you here, to the store?"

"If I didn't know better, I'd think you were interviewing me."

"What can I say? You're a longtime favorite subject." Awkward. Very awkward. He doesn't seem to mind, even as I shrink a little and wonder what it is about him that turns me into a tongue-tied kid.

"I started working here when I came home. I needed a job with flexible hours, and the guy who owned the place was understanding. Before I knew it, I was the manager. And eventually, he decided it was time to retire. He had a choice, sell the place and let it become another gift shop, or let somebody take it over."

He deepens his voice, thrusting his jaw forward. "He made me an offer I couldn't refuse."

I fight to keep my laughter bottled. "Your Brando impression still needs work."

"Hey, at least you knew who I was quoting. Anyway," he continues, chuckling, "here we are. A couple of years back, I knocked down the wall that used to separate the store from the back room and turned it into a café."

I look around at the half dozen tables and the row of stools lined up in front of the counter. "This was all storage?"

"Right, and it was a waste of space. Business exploded once I gave people a reason to come in and hang around. I make sure to send the old guy pictures every once in a while so he sees how well things are going while he's fishing in Florida. I even …"

When he trails off, I lean in, eager for more. He could talk all night, and I don't think I would get tired of it. "You what?"

"I took a baking class over the summer." He jerks a thumb toward the now empty display case. "I started making my own quiche."

To say I'm impressed would be an understatement. "Look at you," I murmur with a grin, folding my arms and seeing him through new eyes. "You've always been very hands-on, though. That much, I remember."

His eyes lock onto mine, and a delicious little shiver runs up my spine. "Yes, ma'am. I sure am."

"And I've always liked that."

If it gets any hotter here, I'll burst into flames. Or maybe that's just me. It's been a long time since I've flirted, and even longer since I've flirted with him in particular. It's like sliding into an old pair of shoes, though. I forgot how comfortable it is.

"What do you say?"

"What do I say about what?"

"Would you like to try one?"

"Are you kidding? Nothing could stop me." He laughs softly, bending behind the counter and fiddling around before straightening up, now with a beautiful quiche balanced on one hand. He frees it from its many layers of plastic wrap, then slides it into the small toaster oven on the back counter. "It will only be a few minutes."

He's true to his word. It's only a few minutes before he's joined me at the table, the quiche between us. As soon as he lifts a large slab from the plate, it's clear he knows what he's doing – the crust looks flaky and buttery, while the aroma of feta and onion makes my mouth water. There's a hefty handful of spinach in there, too, but not so much that it overpowers the other flavors. Mitch watches me as I chew my first bite. Part of me wants to play around with him a little, keep him hanging. But I can't help it. It's too delicious. "Oh, you're kidding. This is ridiculous. You should open a bakery."

"Let's not get ahead of ourselves. I finally got the hang of keeping this place running smoothly." He takes a bite of his own, his brows lifting as he chews. "Yeah, not bad."

"You're being too modest. This is fantastic. Thank you for sharing it with me."

"Hang on a second." He reaches across the small table and without warning touches a finger to the corner of my mouth. "You had a crumb."

Did I? Maybe I did, maybe I didn't. What I care about is the tingle that starts at the point where he made contact and races through my body, ending in a pool of heat in my core. It's so easy with him. So natural. When he leans in across the table, it seems inevitable that this would end in a kiss. It's why I lean forward, ready to meet him halfway.

Until there's a knock at the front door.

He groans while my heart sinks. "You have got to be kidding me." He snickers ruefully before he gets up, frowning a little, but heading to the door anyway. "Sorry, we're closed for the evening."

"Oh, please." It's a woman's voice, and she sounds nearly frantic. "He's been talking all day about a new dinosaur book, and I promised we'd come and get him one, but I had car trouble and needed a tow, and we've had a

Forest of Silence

really rough night. Please, it will only take a minute. He just wants to pick out a new book before we get home."

It's none of my business, but I can't help watching craning my neck a little to see around the rows of bookshelves. There's a woman who can't be much older than me holding the hand of a little boy who's maybe three or four years old. He's adorable, but he looks exhausted. Like his mama.

"Okay. So long as it's only a couple of minutes." He opens the door a little wider so they can slip past him, and I grin myself as I go back to my food. I'm still grinning once he's rung up the sale and locked the door, this time pulling down the shade in front of it like he's sending a message.

"You really haven't changed," I muse when he drops back into his chair with a weary sigh.

"What do you mean?"

"Try as hard as you want, but you're still a softie at heart." Not that that's a bad thing. In fact, it might be the best discovery I've made since I got back to town.

Chapter 13

I should have expected the welcome I would receive in the morning, when I tiptoed out of the guest room in hopes of escaping before Mom got up … only to find her waiting for me in the living room, where I can't leave without walking past the doorway. She's still in her pajamas and robe, her feet encased in a pair of enormous fluffy slippers. She wasn't sitting there when I came in from my run, and I hoped I'd miss her. I don't have it in me today to discuss my personal life. There is hardly anything to talk about, anyway.

"Good morning." She sounds irritatingly chipper. The knowing note in her voice doesn't help matters.

Forest of Silence

"Good morning to you. You're up awfully early."

She lifts a steaming mug. "There's coffee in the kitchen if you want some."

"No, thanks. I might grab some at the station. I want to speak to the captain right away."

"You think you have a lead?"

"I'm not sure." And that's as much as I feel comfortable sharing.

"You got in late last night." She can't hide her smirk behind that cup. I can read the woman like a book.

"Not very. Though you were in bed by the time I got here."

"I didn't think there was any need to wait up. What's wrong with that?"

"I was sort of expecting you to be ready to pounce on me. I should've known you would do it this morning, instead."

"What was I supposed to do?" She sets the cup down on a coaster, then throws her hands into the air. "The boy wanted your phone number. I happen to have it. He said it was important."

"And somehow, you came to the conclusion that I would be home late, and there would be something worth discussing this morning. You act like I haven't known you my entire life."

"Did something happen?" She can't be bothered to pretend the idea doesn't thrill her. "He's still single. He's a business owner. He's a nice, steady guy – and he's cute as a button. He's the whole package."

"I cannot discuss this with you right now." I can't help laughing, but the sentiment remains the same. "Maybe sometime, when I have the mental and emotional bandwidth, we can discuss my personal life and who should be part of it. Right now, I need to get down to the station." As an afterthought, I add, "But thank you for giving him my number. He may have helped push the investigation forward. And that is all I'm going to say," I insist once her mouth falls open like she's ready to drown me with questions.

There are worse things in the world than having a mother who cares, even if the mother in question has a funny way of sticking her nose in right where it doesn't belong. But then I guess that's what all mothers do. Maybe there's a handbook they give out in the hospital. *Welcome to motherhood. Here's how you can meddle in your child's life.*

The fact is, we've spent too many years on the periphery of each other's lives. I won't take her presence for granted now.

One positive development brings a relieved smile to my lips as I walk down the steps and head for the car. There is not a cloud in the sky this morning, and it's still early enough that brilliant rays of pink and golden light linger in the eastern sky. I love mornings like this. My pre-dawn run was exhilarating thanks to the crisp air that for the first time in two days doesn't hold so much as a hint of moisture. It's cool and dry and gorgeous, which goes a long way toward lifting my spirits a bit as I back down the driveway and turn onto the street.

Would it be hopelessly juvenile if I stopped by the bookstore to say good morning to Mitch? He must have the cafe open early, serving those who like to grab their coffee and a copy of the morning paper before heading to work. The idea is almost tempting enough to make me slow down as I roll past the store, but at the last second I lean a little heavier on the gas, instead.

It isn't that I don't think he would enjoy the visit. It's not that I wouldn't like the chance to flirt a little, to get my blood pumping and my heart racing in a way not even the longest, fastest run can do.

But that isn't why I'm here. There's too much at stake, too many lives involved. Mitch is a welcome diversion, but a diversion nonetheless. I can't afford to let him knock me off my game.

So instead of picking up a latte from his cafe, I order a cup from the truck parked in front of the station. As an afterthought I grab a second cup, along with a couple of muffins. Something tells me the captain might need it.

A knowing whistle sounds out once I'm inside and heading back to the corner office where the captain has probably been since before the sun rose. "Look at this. Teacher's pet." I don't bother giving Andy Cobb the benefit of an icy stare, since that's clearly what he wants. He's the sort of person who needs attention, be it positive or otherwise. And I doubt any coldness from me would make a difference, anyway. Knowing laughter rings out around him. He got what he wanted. Once again, I look like a fool while he sits and laughs like a hyena.

The captain doesn't laugh. He looks like a man adrift in open water who just caught sight of a life raft once I enter his office and place the cardboard cup carrier on his desk. "Bless you. How did you know this was just what I needed?"

"Lucky guess." I leave a cup and a muffin on his desk, then take the rest for myself before sitting in a rather uncomfortable molded plastic chair. "Did you have a chance to look over what I sent?"

"There isn't much context here." He scratches his head, gesturing toward his screen. "Just an email saying *take a look at this*. What am I taking a look at?"

Sometimes I forget others don't live in my head the way I do. To me, my message made all the sense in the world. "I was sort of in a hurry to send it to you this morning. I would have done it last night, but I didn't want to disturb you."

"You wouldn't have been disturbing me. If anything, I might have thanked you for a distraction from trying to fall asleep." This time he rubs his eyes with both fists. "I can't seem to sleep especially when I force myself to try."

I make it easier on him, explaining the context of the screenshots I emailed. "I asked Mr. Dutton to provide a few screen grabs for me. They're the clearest images the camera picked up."

Captain Felch studies them now. He tips his head one way, then the other, before blowing out a sigh. "It's not very clear, is it?"

"It's plenty clear. It's just he never really shows his face to the camera."

"Deliberately?" He looks away from his screen, arching an eyebrow.

"That's what I was wondering. It could be. He could have noticed the camera up there and took pains to avoid it. But that would hint at premeditation, and the guy's been coming in more frequently for weeks. Ever since Camille started working there, according to the timeline Mitch helped me put together."

"Considering we have yet to find her, this guy could be the sort who planned this well in advance." This time, I hear the fatigue he can't hide. "I've got just about everybody in town breathing down the back of my neck, demanding we find her. I've never seen anything like this. A case like this, you find the kid a day or two later, shacked up in some hotel. Or…"

He doesn't need to finish his thought.

Or, they end up dead in a drainage ditch.

We have yet to get a report from the medical

examiner on Lila, but it should be coming along soon. I can't help but hope there's a way to tie the girls together, some sort of clue that can lead us to Lila's killer. It's not usually that simple— that's the way it works out in the movies. Sheer coincidence ties a pair of cases together, helping law enforcement track down the culprit that much sooner.

Sometimes, the kid who was missing in the first place ends up being alive. Sometimes, the good guys get there just in time.

But this isn't a movie, no matter how much I wish it were. I'm sure Camille's parents feel the same way. "It could be we're dealing with some-body who's planned this for a long time. I'll ask around, see if anybody recognizes the guy's profile."

"You know what you could do," he suggests before gulping down what's left in his coffee cup. I'm pretty sure he's living off caffeine at this point, with the bags under his eyes serving as mute testimony to the very little bit of sleep he's getting. "Go over to the school. See if any of the office staff recognize him. It could be he's got a kid at the school— that could be his way to get closer to Camille. Maybe she's friends with his daughter or niece or something, and she was able to feel more comfortable with him because of that connection."

"It's worth a shot. I mean, it could turn out to be nothing. There're plenty of creeps out there who end up being relatively harmless."

"But I'm sure they teach you at the Academy that it's never a good idea to let a lead go unexplored."

"That's one of many lessons they teach, yes."

I'm on my way out of his office when he stops me. "Keep your phone on. We should be getting that report from the M.E. by the end of the day. They know they need to expedite."

"It's always in my pocket," I tell him before heading out. This time, I allow my gaze to sweep over the room. Let them laugh at me while I'm looking them in the eye. A few of Andy's buddies pretend to be very involved in whatever they're working on— it's nice to see anybody getting work done around here. From everything I've witnessed, I wouldn't be surprised to find out they sit around and swap stories all day rather than doing real police work.

At this rate, I may as well enroll in school again. That's how it feels after I pull up for the third day in a row in the visitor lot before heaving a sigh. The memories that threatened to bury me when I first arrived are softer and further away. They aren't as immediate anymore. I can breathe easier. I can focus on the task at hand ... even as my eyes stray toward the ice rink, where Danny Clifton's life took an unexpected turn last night. I force myself to look away, continuing toward the school.

A few last-minute stragglers run past me and up the steps, and inside I hear the ringing of the bell, signaling that the first period is about to start. I've made that run many times, sprinting full out in hopes of avoiding a tardiness demerit.

Instead of doing my best fifty-yard dash this time, I hang a right once again and head for the main office. It seems like the best place to start. If I'm unsuccessful, I'll have to widen my search. Maybe I'll visit some of the businesses on Main Street, ask if anyone recognizes the man from the cafe footage. I doubt Mitch's place is the only business he ever patronized. Someone has to know who this man is.

Unfortunately, the receptionist is not one of those people. "I'm sorry," she offers with a pained grimace. "I've never seen him before. Maybe Mrs. Cartwright would recognize him."

Considering the name on the desk reads Mrs. Cartwright, I'm a little confused. "And that isn't you?"

"Oh, no. Sorry. I'm only filling in for her while she's out for the day."

"I see. Maybe some of the other ladies in the office will recognize him."

"Can you sign my slip, please?" I didn't hear the kid who now almost jostles me in an attempt at getting the woman's attention. He thrusts a piece of paper her way. "So I can give it to Mr. Wright when I get to class."

Out of nowhere, he looks down at my phone, sitting on the counter. "Huh. It's Mr. Schiff."

"Excuse me?"

His fair cheeks redden like he wishes he had kept his thoughts to himself. "I was saying that looks just like Mr. Schiff."

"You know Mr. Schiff?"

"Yeah."

"From where?"

"He's my social studies teacher."

Chapter 14

I'm glad the weather is as nice as it is today, even more appreciative than I was when I left the house. It gives me the opportunity to stand outside and take a few deep, bracing breaths as the shock of my latest discovery wears off. There was a moment in there where I thought my head might explode. There I was, already seeing myself going door to door all day, asking for any hint of recognition. I imagined this taking hours. I may even have prepared myself for the very real possibility that it would go nowhere, that I would never find who this man is. It's a thin lead, anyway.

At least, it was. Now I know the contact between Camille and this man wasn't merely accidental. He knew her from school.

And the implications are explosive.

In for four. Hold for four. Release for four. I stand in the shadow of the large, brick building, practicing breathing slowly to center myself. This is not the time to let my imagination run away with me. It could be a completely innocent coincidence. A teacher runs into a student he enjoyed teaching. A student recognizes the teacher and feels she has to be on her best behavior— cordial, polite, that sort of thing. No doubt it's completely common and totally innocent.

No matter how the back of my neck prickles. Cases aren't built on hunches. There's a lot of work to be done.

The first matter, getting permission to speak to Mr. Schiff during the school day. I throw back my shoulders and lift my chin, prepared to face the resistance of a concerned school administrator.

Though as it turns out, once Principal Lewis finally has time to speak to me, there isn't much resistance at all. "I know everyone around here is on edge," she murmurs after closing the door to give us privacy. "And if there's anything we can do to help, by all means. Tess and Brian are family to us, and Camille doubly so. It would be one thing if she were just a student, but the child of two of our most popular and beloved teachers? It's a nightmare. The sooner we find her, the better for everyone."

"I hope you understand I'm not here to accuse anyone."

"Of course." It seems strange that her lips should twitch like she's trying not to smile when she sits down at her immaculate desk. I can't quite get a read on her— at least until she sighs and shrugs. "I'm sorry, but I can't help remembering having you in here before. I was only the vice principal back then, going by my maiden name."

"I remember. Miss Greene."

"That's right. It's strange," she muses, giving me an appraising look. "You get used to watching students get older. You see them graduate. You might run into them in town during holiday seasons when they're back home for break. But you don't expect to find one of them coming to your office as an FBI agent. That is so impressive."

"Thank you. It's a little ..." I can't find the right word as I take in everything around me. The room is so much the same, it's uncanny. The only thing that's changed is the framed photos and personal touches she brought with her when she was promoted. Otherwise I could be sixteen again, sent to the office after I got caught making out with Mitch in the girl's bathroom when I should have been in class.

Edward Schiff has a free second period, as it turns out. "You'll find him in his classroom here on the first floor. If he gives you any resistance, let him know I sent you."

Resistance, huh? An interesting choice of words. Why would she assume that? "Thank you so much for your cooperation on this."

"Whatever it takes, and I mean that."

The bell rings and we exchange a knowing smile. "I think I'll hang out in the outer office until traffic dies down."

"Not feeling adventurous today?"

"My bones are a little more brittle than they were when I was a student here. I'm afraid I'll get knocked down and trampled."

Once the bell for second period rings, I head for Mr. Schiff's classroom. Funny, but I feel sort of awkward walking down the hall without a pass. The soles of my shoes are silent against the tiled hallway, meaning Ed Schiff is unprepared for the soft knock I place against his door.

He jumps a little and coughs when I appear

in his doorway. "I'm sorry. I didn't mean to startle you," I offer. He's sitting at his desk, eating a sandwich out of a brown paper bag, sipping from an open can of Diet Coke.

"That's all right. Please, come in." He reaches for a napkin to wipe his mouth, and the sight of his sharp profile outlined by the sun pouring in through the window beside him confirms it. This is the man. He's in his mid-forties, with a touch of gray in his close cropped, light brown hair. He's wearing the same sort of polo and khakis he was wearing in the video clip Mitch shared with me. Not an unattractive man — really, he's sort of average looking, the kind of guy you could easily walk past and not notice.

But when he smiles in an awkward, self-deprecating sort of way, I can imagine at least a few of his students developing a crush. It really doesn't take much for a teenager, after all. What can I do for you, miss ..."

"It's Agent Forrest, actually."

I cross the room slowly, watching him as I approach. I want him to feel comfortable, which is why I take my time. There's no urgency here. I'm only asking questions. Should I mention the video yet? No, let's see how he handles this first.

Maybe he'll dig a hole for himself and fall into it and make my job a lot easier. Something about this has to be easy, eventually. I need to believe that.

Understanding dawns and his heavy brows lift. "Of course. I heard there was an FBI agent asking questions about Camille. I assume that's what brings you here."

"Yes, I'm trying to get an idea of the sort of student she is, and whether anyone had an inkling of something going on under the surface."

He folds his hands on top of the desk and I notice he doesn't wear a wedding ring. "Any clues so far?"

"Teenage girls are an enigma."

He offers a knowing chuckle, nodding his head. "Aren't they? I don't have children of my own, but I have the challenge of watching them grow up in my classroom."

"I bet that is a challenge. I remember some pretty tough kids back in my day. They didn't make it easy for anybody to get close to them, including their teachers."

"Camille has never been one of those kids."

"Do you know her well?"

"I had her in my class last year. Straight A's across the board. A delight."

"That aligns with what I've heard so far about her. Do you mind if I record our conversation? Just routine. In case I need to look back on something you mentioned. It might not seem important to you now, but it could prove otherwise later."

His brow creases ever so slightly and only for a moment before smoothing out again. "Be my guest. Whatever I can do to help."

I set my phone on his desk and hit record before clearing my throat. "Mr. Schiff, aside from having Camille in your class last year, did you spend any time with her this year?"

"Sure. I'm her coach on the debate team."

"Oh, I see. So you did cross paths more than once this fall."

"It's not easy, mustering the energy to coach a bunch of kids after you've already been in school for hours and you know there's tests to grade when you get home."

"I do not envy you. Compared to her behavior last year, did you see any differences with Camille this year?"

He swallows hard, then takes a sip of his soda before answering. "How do you mean?"

"You know. A change in attitude, maybe? A change in behavior toward you or her friends."

He purses his lips thoughtfully. Is he really thinking about it, or is he stalling? I have to be careful not to jump to conclusions, but I also need to consider all angles here.

"No." He shakes his head before shrugging. "Honestly, I can't think of any difference in her between last year and this year. She was the same bright, respectful, conscientious girl. A diligent student, and she took debate seriously, too."

"You mentioned the hours spent after school. How late would you say the kids stuck around, on average?"

"If we were prepping for a debate against another school, we could stay as late as six or seven sometimes."

"And that's the entire debate team? Or just Camille specifically?"

He blurts out a sharp, disbelieving laugh. "The entire team, of course."

"And about how many kids would that be?"

"Gee, last I counted, there are seventeen kids on the team."

"I see. This must be hard on them, too.

Spending all that time together, I mean. You kind of start to feel like a family."

"That's exactly right. Most of the time, the kids would pool their money and order pizzas so we could have something to eat during practice. They would sit and joke, you know how it is." He chuckles. "They would get on my case for trying to squeeze in a little work during those breaks."

"So, they considered you one of them?" It takes effort to keep my voice light, jovial.

"Kids can be brutal, but they're also accepting. But there is a line," he adds with a comical grimace. "A piece of pizza can turn into fraternizing."

"And that's it? I mean, that's all the time you ever spent with Camille outside of last year's class?"

"Yes, that's it. I might not have much free time, but it's mine."

That does it. That's what I wanted him to say. To deny seeing her outside of school. "You mean you never saw her down at the bookstore in town? You never ordered coffee from her?"

He sits upright like a jolt ran through him. His friendly joking nature is nowhere to be found. "What are you trying to insinuate?"

"I was only asking about security footage I reviewed from the bookstore cafe. The owner tells me he's seen you around there quite a bit, and you're usually chatting with Camille."

"Is there a law against that?"

"No, sir. But you neglected to share that with me, so I thought it was worth bringing up."

"I don't see what you are getting at." Until now, his sandwich has sat forgotten, but now he picks it up and takes a big bite.

"I'm only trying to clarify. Did you forget seeing her at the cafe?"

"I didn't bring it up because it's nothing. I also chat with the guys at the barber shop sometimes. Other times, I stop in at the hobby store to see if they've picked up any new model trains for me to look at. I live near town, Agent Forrest. And I don't appreciate the implications you're making."

"There was no implication, sir. I'm only trying to clarify."

"Well, I hope it's clear for you now. My relationship with Camille was never anything more than professional. The cafe happens to be somewhere I like to relax after work, or on the weekend. A lot of kids from school have jobs along Main Street."

"I'm sure you're right." I stop the recording and tuck my phone into my pocket. "Thank you for your time, and I'm sorry I took up so much of your break." This time around, he doesn't offer a smile. He only goes back to his sandwich, and I feel like a student who has been dismissed.

Chapter 15

There's one thing I'm sure of as I steer the car out of the school lot, I don't believe that guy. Since I'm driving, I can't take out a notepad to record my immediate impressions, so I hit record on my phone again to capture my thoughts on the way back to the station.

"The subject's demeanor changed when confronted with the hole in his story. His body language became closed off, defensive. The affection he has for Camille is clear, though it seems most everyone who knew her feels the same way. Not sure whether it means anything."

I stop at a red light and watch a young mother push a pair of twin toddlers in a stroller. They're fighting over a stuffed animal. I used to wish Maddie were closer to my age so we could share more things, but now that I'm older, something tells me we would have behaved much like these kids are now.

"Note to self, Look more closely at the recordings Mitch Dutton sent. Look for signs of intimacy. Any touching, leaning close, et cetera." I would bet my next paycheck there's something inappropriate in that footage. The way he talked about the kids and how they want him to take a break with them while they eat their pizza...

He tried to play it off, like those silly kids should know better, but I got a different sort of vibe from his story. He likes being liked. Even if it's by a bunch of kids. That can be totally innocent and harmless. It can also be a recipe for disaster.

I'm on my way into the station, eager to share my impressions with Captain Felch, when he beats me to it by sending me a text.

Captain Felch: We got the M.E. report.

"**A**ny evidence of sexual abuse?" That might be the only remotely professional thing I've heard Andy Cobb say since I arrived. We're sitting along with a handful of others in the conference room, where Felch called us together to go over the medical examiner's findings.

The relief that floods my system when the captain shakes his head is palpable. She might have suffered, but she didn't suffer *that*. "No signs of it. All of her clothing was intact, as well. Wet and muddy, but there were no signs of tearing. No struggle."

"Meaning no bodily fluids," Andy surmises in a sour voice. True, that might have helped us locate the murderer. I can see his frustration. I can't blame him— if anything, I should think along those lines and look at this as a professional rather than a woman who hates the thought of another woman being assaulted.

Still. I'm not going to pout about it. Neither is the captain. "Sorry about that, Cobb. I guess you'll have to rely on good old-fashioned police work instead of a DNA test." I lower my head, biting my tongue to keep a straight face. From the sound of it, I'm the only one making such an effort, since there's soft laughter coming from a few of Andy's coworkers.

"And the method?" I ask, prepared to make a note.

"Strangulation, as we surmised from the bruising around the neck. The tool of choice was a rope— the M.E. found blue fibers lodged in her skin. Typical nylon rope, the kind you can buy anywhere. Still, it might be beneficial to visit the hardware store and ask if they've sold lengths of rope recently." That sounds about as promising as the idea of going door to door with a slightly out of focus screenshot and asking if anyone recognized the man in the image. Then again, you never know. I didn't expect to have a random student solve the mystery for me. On my notepad, I scrawl, *Hardware store? Rope?*

When no one else asks, I take it upon myself. "Is there an estimated time of death?" It was a rather narrow window, considering the time between the girls having dinner with her and the discovery of her body was roughly twelve hours.

"It's a little tricky, considering the temperature was close to freezing overnight. In that sort of weather, it takes around two to three hours for rigor mortis to begin and another four to six before the entire body is affected. It had not completely taken effect at the time the body was transported to the medical examiner, and that plus the degree of lividity leaves them estimating time of death only a handful of hours before the body was found. She was not there long."

He lays the report on the table, tapping it with one finger. "The condition of the scene where the body was found was of course compromised by the rain and melting snow, meaning no footprints around the scene. The fact there was no mud or grass on the body except along the back half points to the murder taking place in another location before the body was dumped." Right, because otherwise there would have been signs of a struggle, meaning mud and grass stains. Thinking back to what I saw yesterday morning, I don't remember Lila's hands being dirty like they would be if she'd struggled outside.

"Was there any sign of the body being cleaned off prior to being dumped?" Because why not? Might as well cover all the bases. There are a few barely stifled groans behind me but I ignore them. I'm not sure where these idiots got the idea that being thorough means jockeying for approval.

"There was no presence of any cleaning products or chemicals on the body, no. She was dumped as-is."

He clasps his hands in front of him, looking over the room. "That's what we have for now. Meanwhile, Camille Martin is still out there somewhere." Our eyes meet and I nod slightly so he knows I have an update. Instead of asking me to share in front of everyone, he dismisses us. I have to wonder why he wouldn't have me announce an update to the entire task force— then again, I didn't offer it, did I? Only to him.

"I didn't expect you back so soon," he observes once we're in his office. It takes effort to ignore the daggers being stared through the back of my head from outside the room. I know better than to ask to lower the shade over the glass. All that would do is convince everybody we're hiding something. I don't even want to consider the rumors that might start to stir.

"As it turns out, I got lucky. The man who visited Camille at the cafe is Ed Schiff. He's a social studies teacher and debate coach at Beacon Hill High."

"You're kidding."

"I spoke with him. He conveniently forgot to mention the many times he ran into Camille at the cafe. When I questioned him, he clearly didn't appreciate what he took as an accusation."

"What do you think?" He lowers his brow, leveling a hard, knowing gaze at me. "What's your gut telling you?"

I don't have to think about it. "I think he's a liar. And I think I've got a long night of scouring security footage ahead of me."

"You feel that strongly about it?"

"If he hadn't gotten so worked up when I mentioned the footage, I might feel differently. It was more than that, too," I muse, standing with my back to the window. I'm sure that's driving everybody crazy. They can't read my lips or get a feel for what we're talking about if they can't see me. "He struck me as one of those cool teachers. Do you know what I mean?"

"Sure. And they're usually the troublesome ones."

"We had a teacher like him when I was a sophomore. A substitute after our English teacher got sick— a bad reaction to some medication he was on, it kept him out for months. So this really handsome kid straight out of college came in to substitute, and oh, boy."

He chuckles when I roll my eyes. "That bad?"

"So much worse. But there I was, thinking there was something wrong with me for not trusting him. I just had a strange feeling like he enjoyed the attention the girls gave him."

"Let me guess. There was a big scandal."

"Yes, but not here. For some reason, I looked him up a year or two ago, purely out of curiosity. He ended up with a full-time job at a school in Connecticut, but had to surrender his teaching license a few years back. Something about a corruption of minors charge."

"The cool teacher strikes again."

"Not to say every cool teacher is that sort of person."

"Naturally. You think this Ed Schiff is, though?"

"My gut is telling me yes, there's a definite possibility. I plan to look a little deeper into it."

"By all means, if you can find something in that footage, it could go a long way toward helping us." Still, he scowls, shaking his head. "I do hope it's not true. Imagine. The man is a co-worker of her parents. Maybe their friend?"

"I know." I nod my head at Lila's report, sitting on his desk. "There's no way to tell if their disappearances are linked. And if they are, how does Ed Schiff know Lila? She's not from around here, the way Camille is. She's only been in town a few months. They could have crossed paths somewhere in town, but ..."

"It's a thin connection between the two girls." He rubs his temples like he's trying to ward off a headache— and smiles like he's failing miserably. "Is there anything else to connect them?"

"Only Danny Clifton, but ..." I shake my head. "If you're asking what my gut is telling me, I don't think he had anything to do with it. He and Camille were history, and Lila? The kid broke down sobbing when I told him. I won't rule him out, but it's unlikely. Otherwise, I'm as lost in the dark on Lila as I was before."

"It could be that you have to go back to campus, ask some more questions."

"That was going to be my next stop after I checked in with you about the Ed Schiff situation. I'm wondering if there's any footage of Lila's movements around campus after dinner. There must be. A school like that? There's got to be cameras all over the place."

160

I didn't exactly expect him to jump out of his chair with excitement, but I also didn't expect the skeptical look he wears. "Is that not a good idea?" I ask.

"That's not the problem. I'm wondering whether the dean will be cooperative."

"What makes you think they wouldn't?"

"We had an incident a couple of years back, some Hawthorne students tangling with kids from the high school. Petty, juvenile stuff, until an all-out brawl erupted at a Broken Hill football game. We looked through social media posts from a few of the Hawthorne kids who were involved and it was obvious the fight was planned in advance. They went there looking to crack some skulls. Obviously, that's the sort of thing you need to take up with the dean so they can handle punishment on their end. Let's just say he wasn't exactly cooperative. Wouldn't want to upset the parents and the donors, that kind of thing."

"Well, a girl is dead, and the last place she was seen was on that campus. I would think there would be a degree of urgency here, if only to protect the other students."

He lifts his coffee cup in a parody of offering a toast before remembering it's empty and setting it down with a scowl. "I hope for all of our sakes you're right."

Something tells me he's not going to get his hopes up.

Chapter 16

If I were forced to use one word to best describe President Winters, I would have to go with *dour*. I'm fairly sure his lips will disappear if he tries a little harder to press them in a thin, tight line. He peers at me through a pair of horn-rimmed glasses with lenses that make his gray eyes seem enormous. His navy suit is impeccably tailored and sharp, right down to the white handkerchief peeking out from the breast pocket. If I had to guess, the brackets around his mouth and spanning his forehead along with the generous amount of white hair taking over for the few strands of black that remain would leave me estimating his age in the late fifties.

If anyone was born to their job, it would have to be him. He looks exactly the type to manage an elite boarding school such as Hawthorne Academy. Precise to a fault. Serious. Devoted to tradition and routine.

He also looks like a man who would rather be anywhere else but here at this moment. I've barely been sitting across from him for a minute total, yet he's checked his watch three times. *I get the message. You're a very busy man, and I am messing with your schedule.*

"Thank you so much for taking the time to sit with me," I make a point of saying. "I can't imagine the amount of work that must go into keeping a school of this size running smoothly."

"No. I'm sure you can't imagine." My face must register at least a little bit of surprise, because he adds, "As I'm sure I can't imagine the rigors of FBI training."

Nice try, but there's no putting the toothpaste back in the tube. If I didn't already have a clear idea of the man's self-importance, I would certainly have it now. "Yes, they put us through our paces, but it's all with a bigger purpose in mind. I don't want to take up too much of your time, so I'll cut to the chase. The investigation is still ongoing, and I could use a little help with pinpointing Lila's movement the night she disappeared."

"If you have not been able to do that yet with all your impressive training, what sort of assistance do you think I could offer?" Before I can process this, he adds, "I'm sure you understand, Agent Forrest, that we'd rather not have this already unfortunate situation blow up into a scandal."

Well. If he set out to give me his impression of the situation in as few words as possible, he couldn't have done much better. I sit up a little straighter in the leather chair to which he directed me on entering the spacious, comfortable office. It's twice the size of the one I visited in the girl's dorm, but I suppose that makes sense. The man manages the entire school, after all.

"I'm only trying to understand you clearly, so there's no chance of offending you or upsetting things here at the school."

"Respectfully, Agent Forrest, things at the school are already quite upset." The strained face he makes brings to mind the image of a man who wants to make it home quickly because he's already regretting the burrito he had for dinner. "You have no idea how many phone calls I've taken over the past two days. Parents are up in arms, and donors?" He shudders slightly after whispering the word like he's afraid of being caught swearing.

"I'm sorry to hear that." The way he makes it sound, I might as well be responsible for Lila's demise. "It's nobody's intention to cause trouble."

"I'm afraid that's not exactly true." His nostrils flare when he exhales sharply. "Whoever is responsible for this intended to cause trouble, and I'm afraid they were successful. Please, tell me you've found a suspect."

But just in case I might get the wrong idea and think he genuinely cares, he adds, "Otherwise, I'm afraid parents are going to start arriving, ready to pack their kids up and take them home."

In the end, it's all about the academy. Captain Felch will be so glad to know nothing has changed from the last time he dealt with school administrators. "Unfortunately, we haven't yet. I'm hoping I can find something here that will help."

He removes his glasses, then pulls the handkerchief from his pocket to wipe them. "Exactly what do you think we can provide?"

"Security footage, specifically. I noticed as I walked through campus that there are cameras mounted just about everywhere. There must be footage documenting Lila's movements the night she disappeared. Her friends left her at the cafeteria. I would like to know when she left, and where she went afterward. I need access to the school's footage."

The way he scowls brings to mind a man who just found out he needs a prostate exam. "Surely, you don't expect to find anything on the cameras."

Again, there's nothing I can do but blink repeatedly while trying to understand where he might be coming from. "That was the general idea, sir. I'm only interested in where Lila went after dinner. Whether she returned to her dorm room or went somewhere else. Maybe she was meeting someone. I need to know who that is."

"If it were anyone."

"Of course." At this rate, it will be a miracle if I don't grind my teeth down to nothing by the time this meeting is over. "But we both know something must have happened. Sadly, Lila is dead."

"You do not need to remind me of that."

"And I'm certain her parents would appreciate knowing you offered all the assistance possible," I continue in a low, measured voice.

"Am I remembering correctly? They are both alumni of the school, aren't they?"

With his glasses back in place, it's easy to see his magnified eyes narrow slightly. He gets what I'm hinting at. Granted, I'm not exactly taking pains to be subtle, but I think we're past that point now. The man is determined to protect himself and his school, no matter the cost. At times like this, it's a matter of locating a pain point and applying a bit of pressure. His pain point? Funding for the school. Reputation. Keeping the Board happy.

So what if there's a killer out there somewhere who could very well be targeting other students? So long as nobody blames Hawthorne in any way.

"Unfortunately," I continue, "there's nothing we can do about what's already happened. We can't go back and save Lila's life. What we can do, and what I intend to do, is to ensure the safety of the rest of your students. And I would think the parents and donors would appreciate knowing you've left no stone unturned. That you've cooperated fully."

As a woman in my line of work, I'm no stranger to the appraising looks of men. Sizing me up, deciding who I am and what I'm capable of without knowing me. It goes even farther back than that. I've been scrutinized since I was ten years old. Ever since Maddie. So this is nothing new. If the man expects me to shrivel and shake under the weight of his intense stare, he'll be disappointed. We hold each other's gaze, and mine is unflinching.

He blinks first, both literally and otherwise. "Let's make sure we understand each other. What concerns me most, what keeps me up at night, is the school's reputation. I don't need it getting around that our students are easy targets. Do you understand?"

"Naturally, I understand and I sympathize. I truly do."

"The last thing I need, then, is a report pertaining to a lapse in security measures."

"I understand that, as well. But between you and me, sir, kids are experts at skirting the rules. Haven't you ever noticed that?"

He snorts— it's a derisive sound, almost bitter. It's almost enough to make me wonder if he likes kids at all. Wouldn't you have to, being surrounded by them all day? "Suffice it to say I've met my share of rule breakers over the course of my career."

"This doesn't necessarily have anything to

do with the security measures you've put in place here. If Lila was determined to leave campus that evening, and if she was half as intelligent as everyone makes her out to be, she found a way. I'm not here to point the finger at anyone. I only need to put together a timeline of when exactly she left campus. That's why I'm here today. I need your help."

As a last ditch effort, I add, "The sooner we can wrap this up, the better for everybody. I'm sure you would agree."

The man is between a rock and a hard place, and we both know it. He shifts in his seat like he's uncomfortable but eventually shrugs his shoulders. "You'll have to speak to the guards in the campus security office. They'll be able to pull up the footage you're requesting." He even opens a drawer and pulls out a map. "We are here." He circles the building in which we currently sit, then circles a smaller building at the northeast corner of the school property. "This is where you'll want to go."

"Thank you very much." I'm going to get out of here before either of us says something we'll regret. "And you'll be the first to know of any developments in the case."

He holds up one thin hand to stop me. "I

only ask one thing. Resolve this as quickly as possible so everyone can move on and put it behind them. The sooner this is over, the better."

I don't trust myself to say anything else, so I settle for a firm nod and practically jog out of the room before I get myself into trouble and ask whether he cares at all that one of his students is in the morgue.

Chapter 17

I'm not sure who created this map, but either they need to have their eyes checked or their ability to accurately draw a map called into question. After five minutes of wandering aimlessly, looking at buildings that aren't even on the map, I'm lost in helpless frustration. The song and dance routine I got from President Winters isn't doing much to help my mood. I realize I'm letting that color my outlook, but something about his attitude is stuck under my skin. I will never understand people who can shut down the way he so clearly has. It's one thing for a law enforcement professional to detach themselves from what they see and investigate—that's a defense mechanism. It's the only

Forest of Silence

hope anybody has of keeping themselves sane rather than losing themselves to the darkness.

That is not what I witnessed in that office. It's all about image and money around here.

Up ahead on the brick pathway, I see a man in navy coveralls and a red ball cap carrying a toolbox. "Excuse me!" I jog over to him, still holding the useless map. "Can you tell me where the school's security building is located? This map has me all confused."

He gives me a cursory once over before reaching into his breast pocket and pulling out a pair of wire rimmed glasses. It's a matter of habit, the way I assess him in a practiced glance. He strokes his pointed, clean-shaven chin with stubby fingers. His cheeks are pockmarked like he went through a serious bout of acne as a kid, but he has a ready smile. "Sure. I can't tell you how many people get lost using that stupid thing. I don't see why they don't replace it with an accurate map."

"At least I know I'm not the only one. I was starting to doubt myself."

He does a ninety-degree turn and points straight ahead. "Follow this path around the statue at the center of the quad, then keep going

173

straight. Little red brick building. You can't miss it."

"Thank you for your help." And since I'm already frustrated after wasting time fumbling around like an idiot, I stop just short of running down the path. I can't afford to waste another minute. Camille is counting on me.

If only I knew for sure I would get anywhere with this line of investigation. If the cases aren't connected, I could see Lila's killer in the video footage but still be no closer to finding Camille. Unanswered questions gnaw at my insides and push me to move faster, around the statue of the school's founder and straight ahead as the maintenance man described. The small building is unlike others I've noticed around campus in that there's no grand plaque announcing its name. I guess there aren't any families who want to lend their name to a security office. It's not exactly as prestigious as the library.

At least the man in the office is more helpful than the school's president. "Ah, yes. The FBI agent. I just got a call about you."

I'm sure you did. "Then you understand what I'm looking for."

"Certainly. I've already pulled up the footage from that night." He stands and lets me take a seat, sighing as he does. "A real shame about what happened to that girl. I don't know if you'll believe this, but it has us all broken up."

I murmur my sympathy. "Are you on duty at that time of night?"

"No, ma'am. Strictly day shift." He checks his watch. "Would you mind if I grab a cup of coffee? Figured I'd give you a little time to work alone." When I arch my eyebrow, he shrugs. "You can't get much safer than an FBI agent, right? I can trust you, can't I?"

"Sure." I settle in and he gives me a brief tutorial on how to switch back-and-forth between feeds, how to advance and rewind the playback. It doesn't take long for me to figure it out.

It's nice to be left alone. I take off my coat and hang it over the back of the wheeled chair, crack my knuckles, then settle in with my notepad, prepared to jot down my thoughts.

Right away, I notice Lila's roommates as two of the girls leaving the cafeteria. They are giggling, gossiping— I can't hear what they're saying, but their body language is more than enough. My heart aches when I compare the footage to their tearful, pained expressions when we met in the dorm. They have no idea how their lives are about to be turned upside down.

It's only another few minutes before a slim, dark-haired girl emerges. My breath catches and the strangest sense of past and present overlapping is almost enough to take my breath away. I saw that girl lying in the rain, her body stiff and cold. The girl in front of me is very alive and moving very fast, hands crammed into the pockets of her hooded sweatshirt. She moves with purpose, and I quickly get the hang of switching back-and-forth from one camera to the other so I can follow her across campus. "Where are you going?" I whisper, leaning in close.

Soon, I find out. She went back to her dorm. That doesn't make sense, though— I thumb through my notes, one eye on the footage, before confirming for myself that Lila's badge was not used to access the building that night.

It's so obvious, I slap my forehead when I see it. There was already somebody coming out, and they held the door for her. The girls greeted each other briefly before going their separate ways. That answers that question.

It's only another few minutes before Lila

Forest of Silence

emerges, this time carrying her backpack over one shoulder. I almost forget to breathe as I watch her walking away from the building, taking a narrow brick pathway until she reaches the wide, paved drive leading down to the front gate.

The gates are locked at eight o'clock sharp. The time stamp on the footage reads eight-fifteen. Once the gate is locked, the guard house empties— after all, there's no need for anybody to be on duty when there are no visitors allowed through the gates. Did she know that? If so, that lends itself to premeditation. Well, it didn't take her very long to get her bag together, either, which tells me it might have already been packed up and waiting for her.

But why? "What are you doing?" I ask the dead girl who, after looking back-and-forth— obviously checking to be sure no one was watching— climbs over the stone wall separating campus from the road beyond … and vanishes. There's a lump in my throat that takes effort to swallow back. Why did she have to go?

I keep the footage rolling another minute or two, hoping to find something else … anything else. There's nothing. She walked away, and nobody knew.

The door to the office opens, leading in a blinding flash of afternoon sunlight that startles me a little. "Just me," the security guard murmurs. "Did you find anything valuable?"

That's one word for it. "I think so. Tell me, have you seen anything out of the ordinary lately?"

He leans against his desk, close to where I'm seated. "What do you mean?"

Let me try this from another angle. "How long have you worked here?"

"Six years."

"Alright, so by now, you can tell when something is off, right?" His head bobs up and down. "Is there anything like that? Somebody hanging around campus who shouldn't be? Maybe somebody creeping around nearby? Anything suspicious."

"Well, as you know, any visitors to campus have to sign in at the guard house." He scratches his jaw, his brow creased in concentration. "You know, it's funny. Now that I think about it, there was a truck."

I have to consciously calm myself down. It's easy at a time like this, when the clock is ticking and answers are few and far between, to grasp at anything that seems remotely like a lead. "What kind of truck?"

"You know, a work truck. Not one of those fancy, flashy things. The sort of thing a contractor would drive. That's what I assumed, especially since I saw them drive past the gate a few times, here on the monitor." I move out of the way so he can pull up the footage, and I see what he means. It's an old, nondescript truck, and unfortunately, the angle of the camera doesn't allow for a clear image of the license plate.

"And it always slows down a little when it passes the gate?" I ask after rewinding and rolling the footage a few times.

"Yeah, and then it hit me there were never any tools or equipment in the back."

"So they're not doing work around here."

"So I figure. And I mean, they do have those signs out there, telling people to slow down. I told myself that's why the truck kept slowing. But hardly anybody ever follows those signs—it's not like the kids walk around outside of campus, right?"

"Right. This isn't like an elementary school yard or anything like that, where a kid might bolt into traffic."

"Exactly. So yeah, it's a little suspicious, but I guess that's not what you were looking for."

"I can't discount any lead." Even so, it's not much of anything I can use. "Thank you for your time, and for the use of your equipment."

"Anything you need, and I mean that. I sort of take it personally, that girl going missing. Even though I wasn't on duty at the time."

"We can only do so much," I remind him, noting a wedding ring on his finger. Kids Lila's age, maybe. I wonder if he asks himself how easy it would be for one of his kids to vanish into thin air.

Though if he asked me, I would tell him what I know from experience. It's way too easy. It can happen when you least expect it.

Chapter 18

"Absolutely not. I can't allow it."

I'm going to need some serious dental intervention by the time this is over. I can hear my teeth grinding together as I stand in front of President Winter's desk once again. "I'm only asking whether I can speak to Lila's friends again. They were understandably distraught when I first visited, and at the time, I wasn't sure of the direction my questions should take. It was a very vague, first impression sort of interview."

"An interview which should never have taken place to begin with." He wipes his glasses, scoffing. "And I made sure our Dean of Girls is well aware of my feelings."

I hate to think of a nice lady getting into

trouble, but I have bigger problems now. "Sir, I am an FBI agent conducting an investigation."

"Into the disappearance of a girl with no ties to this school." He sighs while sliding his glasses back into place, almost as if he genuinely feels sorry. "If you couldn't get the answers you needed, I'm afraid that's not my problem."

There go my teeth again. It's bad enough the man kept me waiting for more than an hour outside his office for the opportunity to speak with him again. An hour I spent frantically emailing my latest discoveries over to Captain Felch and explaining the hold up. An hour wasted while Camille is still out there somewhere.

"With all due respect." I stiffen my spine and roll my shoulders back. It's a move I learned a long time ago, a slight change in posture that always serves to give me a little extra confidence when I can feel it slipping away. "I would never walk into your office and tell you how to do your job, sir. And unless you've trained in law-enforcement and how to investigate a case …"

When he waves a hand, it's not only my confidence that's slipping away. It's my self-control. I cannot afford to alienate this man, but he seems determined to make sure I do just that. The audacity! Imagining he knows the first thing about how to approach a situation like this.

"Yes, yes, I'm sure it's very layered and what have you. It does not change the fact that the last thing these girls need at a time like this is constant pestering from the police. They've been through trauma. Why rehash it?"

"Is the possibility of finding Lila's murderer not enough?"

"I hope you're not insinuating the school does not care to uncover who is behind this."

And if I did? He's certainly not doing much to change my mind. "No, sir. That's not what I'm driving at. But what I saw on that footage gives me a reason to believe Lila was planning to run away."

He scoffs, shaking his head. "Lila was the textbook definition of a fine student, and a reliable" young woman."

"Yes, from all reports, that's exactly who she was. But the footage doesn't lie, President Winters. I watched that girl climb a wall to get out of here with her backpack slung over her shoulder. Now, if that doesn't hint strongly at pre-meditation, I don't know what does. I'm hoping one of the girls can shed a little light on this. Was Lila going through emotional problems? Was she feeling overwhelmed? I know it might seem like I'm grasping at straws, but you never know when the slightest bit of information can unlock an entire case. I can't afford to leave any stone unturned."

Anyone would think the man was the most tragic, ill-used person ever born. His heavy sigh seems to come straight from his soul. "That's very compelling, Agent Forrest. Now let me explain to you what I'm going through."

Did I ask? No, I can't afford to voice that little quip, no matter how much I wish I could see his stunned reaction if I did. I've had about all I can take of his snide attitude.

"The fact of the matter is, Agent Forrest, we're dealing with a bunch of minors here. Now," he continues, wearing a sickly smile that turns my stomach, "I think you know, as well as I do, how important it is to get a parent's permission to question a minor."

"None of these girls are under suspicion. They aren't being questioned the way a suspect would."

"Again I say, you will need parental permission to question any of our students from here forward."

"In other words." Folding my arms, I narrow my eyes at him. Why not? He's already made it clear we're at odds. "You've already spoken to some of the parents."

"Some?" His hand shoots out and closes around a stack of slips. Phone messages jotted down by his assistant. "Every single one of these papers represents a furious phone call I received from one or both parents of one of our students." He uses his thumb to fan the papers like he would a stack of playing cards. "Every one is a call I had to return. I wish we had the time for me to go through every insult I've endured today. Every threat I've been forced to listen to. I am the most incompetent man to ever run this school. I am determined to put their children at risk. I do nothing to stand between their precious, innocent kids, and the big, bad wolf."

He flings the papers onto his desk, where they scatter haphazardly. "By all means. Be as disparaging as you like. While you're at it, try to understand a position other than your own. My job is at risk. My family's future. The future of the school— I would say eighty percent of those calls included a threat of withdrawing donations, along with their students. You are not the only one fighting a battle."

I keep my gaze lowered, focused on those messages, while I take and release a slow, deep breath. This is getting me nowhere. "I guess there's no use in asking whether it would be possible to get parental permission to speak to Lila's roommates."

"Your guess would be correct. Their parents are uninterested in involving the girls any further in this investigation."

"That is ridiculous. I'm sorry, but it is."

There's an instant— a split second, no more than that— when the imperious mask he wears crumbles enough for me to see the human underneath. He must be exhausted, maintaining that air of stoicism. "It doesn't matter what we think of it," he murmurs in a much softer voice. "Whether we agree or not. There are rules that must be followed, and this is one of them."

"Very well." Because fighting any harder would be a waste of time, and I've already wasted enough of that today. It's already fully dark outside the office windows. "I'm sorry to have taken up so much of your busy schedule."

But as I walk out of the room, I pause and look back over my shoulder. "As a professional courtesy, let me give you a heads up. Eventually, it's going to come out that Lila left campus by climbing over a wall in plain sight of one of your security cameras. Why didn't anybody catch that? There are going to be more questions very soon."

"I don't suppose I could convince you to keep that part out of public knowledge?"

"Like you said. My hands are tied." Then I leave before he can have the last word.

I want to hit something. I want to make something hurt. Because right now, I am hurting, bleeding out. It seems like every direction I look in, there's another wall in front of me. I step out into the cold night, breath rising in a fog around my head. The air is so clear and so biting that it burns a little when I force a deep breath into my tight chest. I welcome the sensation. It centers me, it cools off some of the raging heat threatening to consume me.

Growing up in Broken Hill, you learn the difference between the haves and the have-nots pretty fast. It's practically part of the school curriculum. There're the wealthy people— residents and tourists alike— and there's everybody else. And it's our job to cater to them, because they keep the town running. If we want a place to live, we need their money.

I'm sure the same goes for the boarding school. If it's going to run, it needs students and funding. And that's more important than anything. It's even more important than bringing a killer to justice, a killer who, for all these parents know, could be targeting one of their kids next. It baffles me. I just can't wrap my mind around that way of thinking. Is there really such a vast difference between the wealthy and the blue-collar?

The site of a security camera mounted close to the building gets me moving. I can't shake the feeling of eyes watching me. I'm sure the president will breathe easier once I'm out of here— for all I know, he's called down to security to make sure I leave. What a shame the security office isn't as on top of things all the time. Somebody might've noticed Lila making a run for it in time for someone to stop her before she made it very far.

By the time I reach my car and do the customary wait for the heater to kick in, one thing is clear, questioning the girls any further might just as easily have led to another wall in my face. Lila was a smart girl. Unobtrusive, the sort who kept her nose to the grindstone. From what I've learned about her, she doesn't strike me as a gossip, somebody who runs their mouth nonstop. Someone as quiet and introspective as her would likely keep her plans to herself. The girls obviously had no clue what she was thinking if they expected to find her studying in their room when they got back from the movie. She had them fooled.

And it could harm more than help if I pointed out she had a plan to run away and they were in the dark about it. One more thing for them to blame themselves over. They might tell themselves there was something they should've seen or interpreted in a way they didn't. That won't help anybody. Nobody needs to carry that sort of guilt on their shoulders for the rest of their lives.

I back the car out of the space and leave the lot, painfully aware as I roll slowly through the front gate that for all any of us know, there could be another girl at the school planning the same sort of escape Lila planned. And without updating the kids on what to look out for and what to steer clear of, there's no way of guaranteeing this won't happen again.

After all, as far as the killer is concerned, they've gotten away with it. And an entire school is in on the cover-up.

Chapter 19

After the day I've had, the last thing I feel like doing is sitting down with my mother and rehashing the details. I probably should have decided what to do before leaving Hawthorne, but it seemed more important to get off campus as soon as possible. Wouldn't want to offend anyone or give Winters the wrong idea.

Now that I'm rolling down Main Street on the way to the old Victorian, something lightens the pressure my foot places on the gas pedal. Does it make me a terrible daughter, wishing I could avoid what's bound to be an exhausting conversation? Do I care right now? I'm a little too beat up, heartsick, disappointed. The captain warned me about the pushback I'd get at the school, yet somehow I didn't quite grasp just how heavy the resistance would be. Impossible to penetrate.

My heart aches a little when I notice the pubs and restaurants as I pass. They're all warmly lit, like a refuge on a cold, unforgiving sort of night. They're exactly what my bruised heart needs – at least, the idea of it. Something warm and friendly and welcoming. Somewhere there won't be a ton of questions and painful memories.

When I see an empty spot at the curb, I take it without a second thought, parking in front of a place called The Tipsy Traveler. It's new – at least, it wasn't here on my last visit, but a lot can happen in three years. It only replaced another, similar business. The decor and the name might have changed, but the idea is the same. Welcoming people traveling through town, making them feel at home.

I'm sure Mom will understand if I don't come home for dinner. Still, I send her a text to give her a heads up before heading inside, just in case she was planning on cooking something when I arrived.

"Welcome!" The girl who greets me at the door can't be much older than Camille. I need to quit thinking about her, but it's impossible.

Forest of Silence

"There's plenty of seating at the bar, or you're more than welcome to take a booth." She waves a menu toward the booths in question, lined up beside the floor-to-ceiling windows facing the street. I'm considering taking a seat at one of them when a familiar face steals the breath from my lungs.

Why in the world would the idea of running away flash in the front of my mind at the sight of Mitch Dutton? It's too late now, anyway, since he looks up from his book and grins once he spots me.

Any hope of a quick escape is forgotten, and not only because it would look terribly rude if I turned on my heel and bolted for the door. It's that grin. It does things to me some men haven't been able to do with their hands. It's magic.

"Just the person I wanted to see." He's like a tractor beam pulling me in, giving me no choice but to take a seat across from him and order a beer. So much for spending a little time alone... but do I really need to be alone?

"Am I?" I tease, because when I'm with him it's so easy to tease. It's easy to be lighthearted and forget how impossible this case is becoming.

Right away his expression shifts to one of concern. "What's wrong?"

"Who said there was anything wrong?"

"Remember?" He points to the spot between his eyebrows, then points at me. "It's better than a mood ring."

"It's been a long day."

His face falls a little, and something unspoken passes between us. I'm no closer to finding Camille than I was before. "I'm sorry. Can I buy you dinner?"

"You can give a girl whiplash, changing the subject like that."

"I know how you get when you're deep into something." He folds a paper napkin in half to use as a bookmark, then closes his novel and moves it to the side. A subtle gesture, but one that isn't lost on me. He's giving me his full attention.

"And how can I get?" I ask, folding my arms on the table and hitting him with a hard stare.

"Would the word obsessive offend you?"

"It doesn't sound like a compliment, Mitch."

"I wasn't trying to compliment you. I'm trying to make a point, though. You tend to forget the little things like eating and getting enough sleep. Remember your eleventh grade science fair project?"

Forest of Silence

"Now why are you going to go and bring that up?"

"It was a great project. What a shame you were too sick and exhausted to present it on the day of the fair."

"I still got an A," I remind him.

"Yeah, along with a doctor's note excusing you from school for two days so you could rest."

"Okay, okay, I get your point. And no, if you're wondering, not much has changed on that front." The fact is, I haven't eaten anything today besides the muffin I got from the truck in front of the station. It might as well have been a year ago— so much has happened since then. No wonder I'm feeling more cranky and irritable than usual.

When our server comes by to deliver my beer, I order a burger and fries to go with it. Mitch either can't hide his relief that I'm accepting his invitation, or he doesn't bother trying. There's something refreshing about that. There's no pretense, no use in playing it cool. He wants to spend time with me. And I would like to spend time with him, come to think of it. I feel normal when we're together. More like myself.

"What are you reading?" I ask when we're

alone again, jerking my chin in the direction of his book.

"Oh, you know. Philosophy. Nothing you'd be interested in."

"Now, how do you know whether or not I'd be interested in it? Give me a little credit."

"So you care about Descartes and Aristotle and Plato now?"

"I didn't say I cared about them, per se," I grumble while he chuckles knowingly. "I mean, I do. They, you know, said some pretty important things."

"Stop. You're murdering me." He touches a hand to his chest like he's wounded. "I'm surprised there's no blood."

"Hey, careful with the M-word," I warn before taking an experimental sip of the pumpkin lager in front of me. It's delicious—slightly spicy, but the sort that leaves me feeling warm inside. Then again, that could just as easily be the effect Mitch's company has on me.

He winces. "Of course. Sorry."

"I'm just teasing."

"If you're teasing, that means you're feeling a little better. I hope you don't mind if I take all the credit." He is entirely too charming for my own good, that much is for sure.

Forest of Silence

"I'd ask how the case is going," he continues, "but something tells me you don't feel like talking about that. Not that I blame you. I'd need a little time to decompress."

"You, sir, are entirely correct." And now I think I might need another beer, especially once our burgers arrive. The aroma of the juicy meat combined with crispy, salty fries makes me wonder if I can get through this without making a complete pig of myself.

There are many things Mitch is good at, and carrying a conversation is one of them. While we eat and drink, we talk more about our lives. Our pasts. He hints around at a relationship that went south a couple of years ago, but he's too vague for me to figure out just how serious things were. Not that it's any of my business, but he is the one who brought it up. I have a hard time imagining anybody being stupid enough to let him go until I remember that I, in fact, let him go.

But I had my reasons. At least, I told myself I did.

I could swear the man reads my mind sometimes. He used to back in the day, too. It's unnerving, but also sort of nice in a way. Except when he uses that power to ask an uncomfortable question. "What happened with us? I always wondered, and you never exactly gave me a solid reason for breaking up."

I owe him this much, and not only because he's buying me dinner. I know from experience what it's like to carry unanswered questions for years. He doesn't deserve that. "I wish I had a good reason, Mitch. I really do. I guess I told myself at the time there was no use in staying together when we were going to be apart. I told myself I was letting you go, so you could enjoy your life without feeling like you were tied down to me."

"You could've just come out and said that, you know."

"I could've done a lot of things, but I was seventeen and in case you forgot, I didn't exactly have the best example of a healthy relationship at home, you know?"

His brows draw together. "That's true."

"Don't get me wrong. That's not an excuse. But I think it plays into it. I was pretty messed up no matter how I tried to pretend I wasn't. Maybe I figured I was sparing you. Again, not an excuse."

"I shouldn't have put you on the spot."

"I didn't see it that way at all. Don't worry about that."

"Because I would've told you, in case you ever wondered, that I didn't want you to set me free or spare me whatever you thought you were sparing me. That wasn't what I wanted at all."

The air is suddenly so thick, I can barely breathe. This is the power he has over me. He can take me straight back to the height of our romance and get me marinating in those feelings all over again even if it's the last thing I ever intended to do.

It comes as a surprise when the lights flicker. I look around, and my surprise deepens when I finally notice how the place has emptied out. "How long have we been sitting here?" I ask, checking my phone. My eyes nearly fall out of my head when I see it's almost eleven o'clock. "I can't believe they didn't kick us out to free up the booth!"

"It's not like we haven't been eating and drinking." He makes a good point. We've switched to coffee and dessert, and I've been picking at a slice of apple cake for the past half hour. I didn't necessarily want it, though it's delicious. I wanted the excuse to spend more time with him.

"At least let me cover the tip," I insist as I reach for my wallet. "The girl deserves it since we took up her table all this time."

"Still thoughtful," he points out as we slide out of the booth. I'm a little fuzzy headed, though I don't know if that's because of the beer or because of the company. There's something humming between us, an energy that can't be ignored. An energy I'm familiar with, goodness knows.

I didn't realize until now, walking beside him out the door of the pub, how much I missed it. How much I missed him. I suppose I never gave myself much of an opportunity to miss him, determined to put him in my rearview mirror and keep him there.

That's something I can't bring myself to say out loud. Something I didn't want to admit even to myself back in the day. He was a symbol of everything I wanted to leave behind— and at an early age, I didn't know it wasn't that easy. It's not like cutting off an arm or leg and discarding it. Mitch, and everything he represents, is part of me, something fundamental. It took seeing him again and spending time together to understand that. Now that I do, I'm not sure what to do with the information.

Forest of Silence

At least, I'm not sure what to do until he asks a question I didn't realize I wanted so badly for him to ask until it comes out of his mouth. "Would you like to go back to my place?" He turns to me, smiling a little in that old familiar way.

"It depends on what you have in mind, Mr. Dutton." I bite my lip to hide a grin, leaning in a little closer to catch a hint of his cologne. "I hope you wouldn't want to take advantage of a girl after buying her dinner."

"Is it taking advantage if the girl looks at me the way you're looking at me right now?" He reaches out and drags his thumb over my cheek like he's testing its softness. It's enough to make me forget to breathe.

"Exactly how am I looking at you?" I can't stop checking out his lips, remembering what it's like to be kissed by him. Is he going to kiss me now? Will I make it out of this alive if he doesn't? Because every breath in my body is tied up in whether or not he'll kiss me, since that's the one thing I need him to do more than anything else. I need him to kiss me until I forget everything for a little while.

I need him to kiss me until I remember everything I tried to forget for so long.

KATE GABLE

He takes my face in his hands— gentle, but firm, stroking my cheeks as he leans down. He takes his time, his eyes searching my face like he wants to be sure this is what we both want.

Which is why I wrap my arms around his slim waist and pull him closer so he knows. If there is one thing in this life I have no doubt about, it's him. How very much I need him right now.

And when his lips finally touch mine and unlock an entire avalanche of memory and sensation and need, there's no question where I'll be spending my night.

Chapter 20

"Somebody's got a spring in her step today."

It takes everything I have not to react to Andy Cobb's barely audible comment, delivered mere moments after I've stepped foot into the station. If I didn't know better, I'd think he's aware that I spent the night with Mitch. There's no way he possibly could. He's only looking for a way to get under my skin — why, I'm still not sure. It's like he decided to make it his life's mission to irk me when we first met.

Do I have a spring in my step? Maybe I do. If so, I have plenty of reasons to. But it's none of his business. Ignore. Be the bigger person. I'm not sure how much more of that I have left in me, but I'll do my best.

KATE GABLE

"Hey, Cobb!" Felch steps out of the break room, a steaming paper cup in one hand. I didn't know he was watching— judging by the unique shade of red Andy's face has become, I'm thinking he didn't, either. "If you want to be a comedian, head down to the open mic night at Charlie's. They have it every weekend. Otherwise, we're here to work. Come on," he adds, raising his voice to be heard by more than just a few of us. "It's time for a briefing. Let's move."

We file into the conference room, and I snag a chair close to the spot where the captain usually stands to deliver his briefings. Our eyes meet as he enters the room, and he rolls his slightly while blowing out a sigh. I lift a shoulder. It is what it is.

"Alright, everybody." The room goes silent when he starts to speak. "Based on the information which Agent Forrest uncovered yesterday, we sent an alert out to all departments across the region to be on the lookout for a truck matching the description of the one that's been spotted circling the Hawthorne campus. We know it's a thin lead, but it's all we have at the moment."

Someone behind me asks, "Any chance of talking to the roommates?"

Felch lifts an eyebrow at me and I clear my throat. "I'm thinking no. The school's president has made it clear that the parents refuse to let their kids talk to law enforcement."

"It's not a surprise," the captain muses with a scowl. "We all know how closed off they are over there. They don't want anything that's going to cast a bad light on them getting out into the public. And they shelter their kids above everything else."

"A bunch of snobs," someone mutters, and the soft laughter following that little remark tells me everybody agrees. So do I, frankly, but I'll keep my opinion to myself.

"It's frustrating, but we know what to expect from them by now. According to security footage, Lila climbed a wall at roughly eight-twenty in the evening while wearing a backpack as if she was already planning on making an escape."

"What have we heard about Camille?" Andy asks. "I thought that's what the FBI was here for." He says it almost jokingly, but it doesn't matter. For some reason, there's still enough ill will that the damage has been done. I hear more than a little bit of faint grumbling and muttering in the aftermath of his remark.

"From what I can tell," the captain fires back, "it's Agent Forrest who has gotten us anywhere with this investigation." He lowers his brow before adding, "Unless you would like to go over to Hawthorne and face down the president and all the nasty threats and phone calls we'll be sure to receive from the parents of the kids over there. By all means."

It's a relief when the briefing breaks up. "I would love to know what I did to irk him so badly," I mutter once the captain and I are back at his office.

He shakes his head and snickers. "Between you and me, I think there are more than a few of my officers who wish they had what it takes to work with the Bureau."

"Really? I figured they just didn't like having their toes stepped on."

"Oh, they hate that, too," he's quick to assure me with a faint grin. "Two things can be true at the same time."

For a man on the brink of exhaustion, he still has a sense of humor. "I was thinking about going back and rattling Ed Schiff's cage again. See if he might have uncovered a few more memories of time he spent with Camille now that he's had a little more time to think about it."

I hardly expected him to leap from his chair and do a cartwheel, but I at least hoped he'd take my suggestion positively. Instead, his brows draw together before he shakes his head. "I wouldn't do that."

"Because?"

"Because we have no connection between him and Lila, for starters." He holds up one finger, then follows it with a second. "Two, there's no evidence linking him to Camille's disappearance. All we know is he took an interest in her. If there was any improper contact, that's one thing, but that still doesn't mean he kidnapped her."

He's right, of course, but I don't have to like it. "I had another idea I wanted to float by you. I want to take a look at Camille's bedroom if the parents will allow me."

He sits back in his chair, his fingers tented beneath his chin, while his lips draw together in a pensive expression. "I'm sure they would already have gone over it with a fine-tooth comb."

"Do you think so? Because I remember back

in the day when I had things to hide from my parents."

Now his lips twitch like he's trying to hide a smile. "Nothing illegal, I hope?"

"Either way, I think the statute of limitations has long since passed. But no, nothing like that," I assure him while we both chuckle. "But you get my idea. I became something of a pro at hiding notes, clothes I wasn't allowed to wear. And yes, maybe a pack of cigarettes every now and then. Kid stuff. But at that age, it meant everything."

"So you think she might've hidden something where her parents couldn't find it."

He's interested. I have him on the hook. "There's a chance. It could be something that sheds a little light on her relationship with her teacher. Maybe something from Danny Clifton – a picture, a letter."

"Kids usually exchange that sort of thing electronically nowadays."

"We did back then, too. I'm not that old," I remind him. "Still, there's a chance, and I don't want to miss any chances. For all we know, there could be something hidden in there that takes us in a completely different direction."

"All right, all right." He holds up his hands

in surrender. "You make a good case, agent. Go forth with my blessing, and let Brian and Tess know you're there with my support, just in case they have any questions."

***

"Oh. Alexis." Tess runs a trembling hand over her disheveled hair before correcting herself. "I mean, Agent Forrest."

"Alexis is just fine." I'm as gentle as I can be, offering a sympathetic smile in the face of her unkempt appearance. She's not at school now. There's no press conference to prepare for. She doesn't have to spend any of her precious energy worrying about how she looks when I'm sure it's taking everything she has just to function at the bare minimum.

"What can I do for you?" she asks while gathering together the sides of her oversized cardigan. There's a stain on the T-shirt underneath it, and I noticed her nails have been chewed down to the quick. Just like Mom's were. Will my subconscious ever stop linking the past to what's happening now?

"Can I come inside?" I ask when she shivers

in the brisk morning air. "If it's not too much of an inconvenience, I mean. I wanted to ask a favor of you."

That question does the trick. It gives her something else to focus on if only for a minute or two. Her sunken eyes clear up, and her posture straightens before she steps back and opens the door wider. "Of course. Come in. I'm sorry, the house is a mess."

"You don't have to apologize." I would offer to help pick the place up if I didn't think it would insult her. Granted, it's dark enough with the curtains closed over the windows to conceal most of the mess. Like walking into a tomb. The TV is tuned to CNN but the volume is muted.

I notice a few wrapped dishes on the table inside the front door, and she chuckles almost like she's embarrassed. "Everyone has been so generous, I ran out of room in the fridge. Maybe you could take something with you?" she asks with a vague wave of her hand.

"Maybe," I reply, even if I have no intention of doing that. The air is thick with sadness, almost too heavy to breathe. "Like I said, I have a favor to ask you. I wanted to know if I could look through Camille's room."

She tucks her hair behind her ears before wrapping her arms around her thin frame. It shouldn't be possible for her to look even thinner only two days after I last saw her, but here we are. She'll be a skeleton before much longer. "Why? If you don't mind me asking."

"I don't want to leave any stone unturned. If there's a chance there might be any little thing up there, I would like to see for myself. I'm not trying to be disrespectful," I assure her, because I feel it needs to be said when looking at the pain etched on her pale, haunted face. "I just don't want to miss any opportunity there might be to find her. Does that make sense?"

She gulps before her head bobs up and down, her chin quivering. "Sure. I get it. By all means. Top of the stairs, the first door on your right."

"Thank you. I won't be long."

"I'll be here." Her laugh is shaky, touched with an edge of panic. "I have nowhere else to be. Just waiting for the phone to ring..."

The desperation in the air is almost thick enough to taste. I hate the sense of uselessness that plagues me as I climb the stairs. It's not enough to promise I'll do my best. I need to bring this girl home. For her sake and her parents'.

First things first, finding out whether the good girl was hiding anything.

Chapter 21

The first word that comes to mind once I've eased open the door is neat. Camille is a very neat person— for a teenager, anyway. There are the typical exceptions, a pair of jeans flung over the back of her desk chair, shoes spread haphazardly across the floor like she kicked them off and let them stay where they landed. There are textbooks stacked on the desk, papers. She made her bed that morning. A handful of small succulents line the windowsill and a few academic trophies are scattered over her bookshelves, placed in between rows of novels. I wonder if she picked any of them up from Mitch's store.

At first glance, this is the typical room of a typical teenager. She even has a few framed photos on her nightstand, including the one her parents used on her posters, holding her puppy. I wonder where the dog is now— I didn't see any signs of him downstairs, but then I wasn't down there for very long.

"Okay, Camille." I unbutton my coat after getting my first impressions. "Let's see what you can show me."

Where did I hide things when I was a kid? Of course, the immediate location that springs to mind is under the bed. Using my phone as a flashlight, I get down on my knees and peer underneath, where I find nothing but a few dust bunnies and an old pair of flip-flops. I lie on my back and shine the light underneath the box spring – sometimes I would use duct tape to secure a pack of smokes I planned on sharing with Mitch, that sort of thing. Nothing.

I lift the mattress next, sliding my hand between it and the box spring, but nothing comes of that, either. I even check the pillows just in case she hid something in the pillowcase. Then I make sure to carefully arrange the bed the way she'd left it. I'm not trying to be disrespectful.

I hate to look through her dresser, but I put on a pair of gloves from my coat pocket and do it anyway. She even neatly folded her clothes

Forest of Silence

and arranged them in tidy rows. This is a kid who thrives on discipline and routine. I certainly wasn't like her at that age, but then, by the time I reached that age, I'd had more than a few challenges to deal with. Such as a mother who was too busy trying to hold herself together after her husband's shocking crime and her daughter's brutal murder to worry about her younger daughter's laundry. Or homework. Or just about anything some days, when the grief was so dark and so impenetrable she couldn't find her way out of it.

In other words, I was on my own much of the time. So long as my clothes were clean, I didn't particularly care about how they were organized.

There's nothing there, not even behind the dresser when I shine the flashlight there. Nothing underneath. I check the closet next, standing on her desk chair to search the top shelf for any hidden clues. And every minute that passes without a discovery takes me one step closer to wondering if I'm completely off base. Maybe Camille didn't have any secrets. Maybe she truly is as good and honest as I've heard.

At this point, I'm not sure if I want her to be

or not. I mean, if she stepped out of line just once and left evidence of it somewhere in this room, it might go a long way toward helping us find her.

Still, after searching between and behind her books, behind the bookcases, along the top of her desk and inside the drawers, I come up empty-handed. Her poor mother is downstairs, puttering around, even muttering to herself. Now I hear the dog running around down there. I don't know where Brian is and I'm not sure if I should ask. Whatever he's doing, I'm sure he's just as lost and despairing as his wife is.

You can't take everything on yourself. Something Mitch said to me this morning before I left to sneak into mom's house like a naughty kid and change my clothes before heading into the station. It's not your personal responsibility to solve everybody's problems.

He used to tell me that back in the day, too. And what he didn't understand then any more than he understands now is that when something so tragic invades your life and changes your trajectory, there is no such thing as not taking everybody's emotions and heaping them onto your shoulders. Just like Mom's peace of mind became my responsibility – not that she ever requested it — it's my responsibility to put an end to the Martins' suffering. It's not a conscious decision. I'm not trying to punish myself. That's how my brain was rewired after Maddie's loss and everything that came after.

I don't want there to be an after for these people. "Come on, kid," I whisper, turning in a slow circle and scanning the room in hopes of noticing something I forgot to check. "Tell me something. Show me what was going on with you." Out of sheer frustration I check her desk drawers again, sort of like the way a person can open the refrigerator door after they have already checked, as if something new will magically show itself.

This time, I take everything out of each drawer and place it on the desk, then go through it all. There isn't so much as a printed photo or a thin notebook where she might have hidden her secret thoughts. My frustration grows as I move from one drawer to the next, finally arriving at the deep bottom drawer.

And that's when I noticed what I missed the first time. I had to empty that deep drawer and look at it critically before seeing the obvious. From the outside, the drawer looks around twelve inches deep, but inside there's only

KATE GABLE

around eight inches between the top of the door and the bottom.

The familiar tingle begins at the back of my neck but I push it aside in favor of feeling around the bare particleboard. Finally, after running my nails around the edges, I find a small depression. It's just big enough to hook my nail around before pulling at it.

Like magic, the board lifts. A false bottom. Hidden inside? I close my gloved fingers around a Samsung Galaxy phone that is definitely not the iPhone her parents purchased for her last birthday.

It looks like Camille had at least one secret she went out of her way to keep.

Chapter 22

"The phone is on its way back to the field office in Boston." There's a grim sense of satisfaction mixed with resigned understanding as I steer my Corolla away from the office of the courier service. "They're our only chance of getting it unlocked. Camille locked it using a six-digit password and biometrics."

"Meaning a fingerprint or face recognition?"

"Right."

"It sounds like somebody wanted to be sure there was no chance of anyone opening it." The captain sighs, and the sound fills my car thanks to the speaker function on my phone. "How did Mrs. Martin take it?"

"She was confused. Naturally, she had no

idea the phone existed. She couldn't tell me where Camille might have gotten her hands on it. This wasn't one of those prepaid burner phones you could pick up at a gas station or convenience store."

"And they're not cheap, either."

"I did a quick search, and they are at least a couple of hundred dollars for the basic model. I'm not sure which model she had, but I can't imagine it was inexpensive."

"Who goes to all that trouble?"

I know which direction my thoughts immediately moved in. "You know what I'm going to say, don't you?"

"Until we can prove Schiff had anything to do with it …"

"I know." And I do. But it's times like this when I hate having to wait. Wasting time, dragging my feet. In the very marrow of my bones, there's a grim certainty Ed Schiff had an inappropriate relationship with that girl. It would not surprise me in the least if there were messages from him on that phone. If the phone number was linked to him somehow, if he were paying the bill for it, we'd be all set.

"I don't need to tell you they know what they're doing at the Bureau."

I roll my eyes, glad he can't see. "Yes, they are pretty efficient." And they should have the phone within the next couple of hours. With any luck, they'll have it cracked by the end of the day.

And Ed Schiff will be in custody.

Another call comes through from an unknown number. "I'll keep you updated," I promise before switching over. "Agent Forrest."

"This is Dr. Olivia Gray, from the medical examiner's office."

I sit up a little straighter. "How can I help you?"

"I found something here I thought you might be interested in. Can you stop by the office?"

Can I? Nothing could stop me. "Give me five minutes," I tell her as I hang a sudden left turn.

"So there's been no autopsy on Lila's body?"

The medical examiner shakes her head as she leads me down a wide, white hallway to her office. "That happens sometimes. We have to abide by the parents' wishes."

"I see."

She leads me into a room much warmer and more inviting than one would expect. There are framed photos on the walls — older photos of a younger version of Dr. Gray along with the trio of curly headed kids, and newer photos of what must be grandchildren. I guess people do whatever it takes to make it through a job like this, where some of the worst examples of what humans can do to other humans might otherwise wear a person down until they are nothing but a husk. We all do what we need to do.

There's a small refrigerator behind her desk. "Would you like a bottle of water?" she asks, opening the door to pull one out for herself.

"No, thank you. I'm fine." I take a seat when she offers one, wondering what we're doing here since she hasn't explained yet. I need to do something about my anxiety. Maybe I'm a little too close to this case for comfort— I can't shake the memory of Tess Martin, how lost she seemed. Like a ghost, still living and breathing, but not truly alive. Her life force has been dimmed. What about Camille's life force? Was she being taken advantage of by someone she and her parents were supposed to trust?

"As you know," Dr. Gray continues, "the cause of death was by all appearances strangulation. Ligature marks, fibers embedded in the skin." As she speaks, she heads for a filing cabinet along with the wall opposite her desk. After pulling a set of keys from the pocket of her blazer, she opens the drawer and withdraws a manila folder and a small, brown envelope. "But take a look at the photos, and you'll see what I dismissed in my original report."

She opens the folder on her desk to reveal a set of large pictures of Lila's face and neck. To think, only hours before they were taken she was with her friends, having dinner, planning to run away. I can see her in the camera footage— walking fast, determined, in a hurry to get somewhere. A girl putting a plan in motion. I can't help but wonder if that sweet kid had time to regret it before someone extinguished her light.

"As you can see, there's the typical bruising around the throat." I nod, my eyes glued to the ugly marks against ghostly pale skin.

She flips to another photo and hands it to me for inspection. "I dismissed this. I shouldn't have, but when you've seen enough cases your brain can make up excuses and explanations from past experience."

She taps the photo with one neatly manicured nail. "This swelling."

Now that she points it out, I notice a small lump roughly an inch south of the marks left from the rope. "I chalked it up to edema resulting from the trauma to her throat, but decided to investigate while preparing the body for release to Lila's parents. There's no discoloration of the skin."

I look up from the image to meet her steady gaze. "Meaning it happened post-mortem?"

"It looks that way."

"What could've caused it?" Right away, the gears start turning in my head. "She was out in the open. An insect? Did something crawl into her throat?"

"There aren't many insects around, not since our first frost."

Now I remember the small envelope which the examiner picks up and opens. From her pocket, she pulls a large pair of tweezers, which she inserts into the opening to withdraw a glass vial.

I lean in closer, holding my breath. "May I?"

I ask, pulling gloves from my coat pocket and pulling them onto my hands. Once I've taken the vial, I hold it up to the light coming through the window over my shoulder.

Inside, there's a stone. "A crystal? A gemstone?" I murmur, examining it from all sides. It's roughly the size of my thumbnail. Rough, unpolished. A blood red color.

"My first thought was garnet," she murmurs. I guess it could be. Regardless, it had no business in her throat. "Once I extracted it, I took note of damage to the tissue of the throat. Like someone had forced it in there."

"A calling card?" That's a rhetorical question, spoken more to myself than to her. The tingling in the back of my neck is almost unbearable, like my skin is sizzling. I don't yet know what it means, but I know it must mean something.

If there were any question in my mind of whether this was some random killing or a premeditated act, that question has been silenced. Only a killer with a plan in mind and a message to send would do something like this.

Chapter 23

"We have the phone."

"Good, I'm glad to know it got there so quickly." I hold my hands out to warm them in front of the car's vents. What was already a frosty day has turned colder, blustery. I can feel the snow in the air. There was nothing I liked better as a kid— snow brought the possibility of curling up under a blanket all day with nothing to do but read while flakes covered the ground. Kids have that luxury. Adults, not so much. Especially not when there's a missing girl out there somewhere. This is not the sort of job where one gets to take a snow day.

"Any idea on how long it might take to open it?" I ask, hopeful.

"You'll be the first to know." Not exactly an

answer to my question, but then I suppose nobody likes being rushed.

"Thank you. You know how to reach me." I end the call before letting out a frustrated growl. I've never been the most patient person, and I've never dealt well with feeling useless. I've always preferred to get things done on my own. Something about the uncertainty of relying on others. My therapist— the one I visited in the early days— called it a defense mechanism. When life hands you something so traumatic and shattering, you might develop what he referred to as extreme self-sufficiency.

In other words, it irks me to no end when I have to wait and trust someone else will get the job done quickly enough for my taste— and to help Camille, wherever she is.

Of all times for a once familiar voice to ring out in my head. *Little girl, you've got to learn to let go sometimes.* He was always so gentle when he chided me for my impatience, all the way back when I was little. Back in the good days which seem so far away I still sometimes wonder if I imagined them.

I should go visit him. The idea leaves my heart feeling heavy, but that's no excuse. I've been in town for days and I haven't yet ventured out to the trailer park my father has called home ever since his release from prison. I dreaded seeing Mom, but Dad? That's an entirely different trauma I carry with me at all times, like an invisible shroud. Some days it feels heavy enough to drag me down. Other days, I can almost forget it's there.

There's no forgetting it now. And I know the guilt would eat at me if I avoided him the entire time I'm in town. Since I'm in a holding pattern until somebody from the field office gets back to me, there's no excuse not to take the drive out to see him.

And if someone gets back to me, that can be a decent excuse for cutting out. When I look at it that way, this might be the ideal time to pay a visit.

I wonder what ten-year-old me would think if I went back twenty years and told her there would come a time when she would dread seeing her father. Mom was always the free spirit, or so she tried to be. Bouncing from one interest to another with boundless enthusiasm and not much in the way of follow-through. Hence the half-finished projects and abandoned hobbies. The house was another one of those flights of fancy that soon turned into more of an investment than either she or Dad were prepared for. I believe that, with time, they might have turned the house into the bed and breakfast of their dreams.

Fate had other plans.

It's like the drive I took into town on my first day, only in reverse. Every turn of the wheels takes me a little further away from the cozy, idyllic heart of town, and closer to what is reality for the people who make the town function. The people who clean up at the end of the day, who do laundry and change bedding and vacuum carpets and pick up after lazy, sloppy tourists. People who tend to fade into the background, people who are often overlooked. And the same wealthy visitors who rely on those essential services are the ones who turn up their noses when they pass through what I am now approaching, a sad, bleak, part of town filled with rundown trailers and abandoned vehicles. In some cases, abandoned dreams.

And my father lives here. My father, who could fix anything— literally and otherwise. There was never a time I went to him when he didn't somehow make me feel better about whatever silly, inconsequential thing was bothering me that day. Not that it felt inconsequential at the time. When you're a kid, everything's a big deal. A friend didn't say hello when you first got to school that morning. You studied hard but only got a B on a test when you were hoping for an A. One time, I left the girls bathroom with a piece of toilet paper stuck to my shoe and was inconsolable for days after my classmates laughed at me.

"They'll forget all about it another day or so," Dad told me at the time, sitting me in his lap and wrapping me in one of his bear hugs. My heart aches when I remember the soft, warm flannel shirts he used to wear. I can almost feel them now, how safe I always felt. They always smelled like coffee and fresh wood shavings and home. He smelled like home.

Until … Before and after … Then and now.

That was before Maddie. Before the trial that drained a little more of my parents' vitality every single day. It wasn't enough that someone stole my sister. They stole my family. They stole the people I knew, and replaced them with lookalike versions who were never quite right. Like that old body snatcher movie. They looked and sounded the same and even had the same memories, but the warmth and the tenderness were missing. Like a house with the lights off inside. Empty. Lifeless.

And that would've been bad enough if it hadn't been for Dad's decision that my sister's murderer got off too easy. It wasn't enough for the man to be convicted and sentenced to spend the rest of his life in prison. That wasn't true justice—at least, not in the eyes of a grieving parent. The day of sentencing, police took him from the courthouse to transfer him to state prison. My father used a gun he'd bought from a stranger whose name we never learned and shot that man on the courthouse steps in front of dozens of witnesses. He didn't care about what came next. He only wanted justice for his little girl.

He was not a good shot. All he did was wound the man and land himself in prison for the rest of my childhood and some of my early adult life. He also lost his marriage when Mom filed for divorce while he was behind bars. He didn't put up a fight.

And the thing is, I understand. Somewhat, at least. When I was a kid, I couldn't begin to comprehend what led him to make that decision. He hadn't even told Mom, probably because he knew she would stop him. As far as he was concerned, a vicious, worthless animal took his little girl away. I've seen countless examples of that reaction in the years since.

But this was my family. My father, my hometown full of people who judged me every time they set eyes on me. I was the girl with the dead sister and the inmate dad. The dad who was so selfish, so blinded by grief that he blew to pieces any lingering hope of pulling ourselves together and moving on. He never considered how it would impact me when he pulled the trigger. Growing up without a father, the one person who understood me best. He didn't think about me.

There are tears in my eyes that I have to blink away so I can make out the tiny numbers on the mailboxes in front of the trailer homes. It's a relief to find Dad's in better condition than the ones on either side. There's no tape covering cracks in the windows, no broken blinds, no garbage bags stacked up against the walls. There are a pair of lawn chairs positioned on either side of a small table on which sits a plant that of course died when the frost hit. The paint looks fresh, too, and there's even a little-fenced off area with a small gate. I'm sure he

Forest of Silence

put that up himself before unrolling a strip of artificial turf that leads up to the front door.

For some reason, that's what hurts the most. Seeing how he's tried to make whatever little improvements he can. He might not be the same man I used to know, but that man is in there somewhere. He's not completely lost.

If anything, that's what gives me the strength to get out of the car and open that little gate, to walk up the strip of turf and knock on the door.

Chapter 24

He's wearing a plaid flannel shirt. That's the first thing I notice once my father opens the door. Yes, I register his shock, the way his mouth falls open and his eyes widen, the way he swallows hard before sputtering. The way his hands comb through his salt and pepper hair, a little longer than he used to wear it back in the day. Even when he rakes it back, some of it falls across his forehead.

"Alexis." His voice is the same, and it unlocks something in me. Something I have tried hard to tamp town, to push away. I'm a little girl again, seeing her daddy for the first time in years.

"Hi, Dad." I clear my throat, then crane my neck to look around him into what appears from here to be a neatly kept home. "I hope you don't mind my dropping by like this."

That's the pin that pops the balloon of his shock. He pulls himself together, standing taller before pushing the screen door open wider. "Are you kidding? I am thrilled to see you! Please, come in, get out of the cold."

"Feels like snow, doesn't it?"

"I was thinking the same thing earlier." He holds out his arms, a little hesitant, I'm sure. I hate that he has to be unsure. I hate so many things I didn't realize bothered me as much as they do.

The hug is awkward, but welcome. What's also welcome is the way he's beefed up a little since the last time we hugged. He was practically skin and bones then, but there's a little meat on his frame now.

"You look good," I tell him, and I mean it, and I'm glad to mean it. There's nothing worse than handing someone an empty platitude for lack of anything better to say.

"You mean since the last time you visited?" There's a hard gleam in his eyes that quickly softens into understanding. "Not that I gave you much of a reason for a repeat visit. You'll be glad to know I made a big change starting that day."

"You did?" I follow him deeper into the modest living room, where a sagging sofa is covered in a clean, striped blanket. I take a seat while he settles into the recliner. It looks like it's seen better days, but it's still in one piece. He always did use everything he had until it fell apart.

"That was the day I took my last drink. Three years sober— I just passed the anniversary last month."

My relief is profound. I have to check myself before overreacting and embarrassing him. "Dad. I'm so proud of you."

He strokes his clean-shaven jaw, and I'm struck by the difference in him. He's aged twice as fast as he might have otherwise. If I didn't know him, I might guess he was in his late sixties rather than his mid-fifties— but he's healthy. Well groomed. The trailer is clean and tidy the way he always liked to keep things in better times. I can almost forget why I was so full of dread in the first place.

"Can I get you something to drink?" he offers, already out of his chair even though he'd just sat down. "I have water, juice, Diet Coke."

Forest of Silence

"I'll take one of those. I could use a little extra caffeine."

"I heard you were in town." Our eyes meet when he hands me the can, and I see the worry in the lines at the corners of his.

"Word travels fast."

"How's it going? I understand you can't give me any details." He sits back down and picks up a mug of coffee from the end table.

"I have a good lead. I'm only waiting on word from the field office before I move forward."

"That's good. I've been thinking a lot about the parents. What they must be going through." He looks down into his cup, his jaw ticking, before he sighs. "I hope everything turns out well for them."

"I'm doing my best. How are you?"

He waves a hand indicating our surroundings. The paneled living room, the small round table separating it from the open kitchen with its outdated appliances and scratched cabinet doors. "Living the dream." He sounds so much like his old self. I can't help but laugh. After a surprised beat, he joins me, and any lingering awkwardness dissolves.

"I'm sorry I didn't come by sooner."

"I understand you're busy. I don't expect you to take time out of your schedule to visit your old man."

"Still. I should've called."

"You're here now. That's what matters." He lets out a knowing chuckle that tells me what's coming next before he says a word. "How is she? I assume you're staying at the house."

"How did you guess?"

There's a twinkle in his hazel eyes. "As if she would let you stay anywhere else?"

"Good point. She's fine. Doing well. Do you ever see her around town?"

He grimaces almost like he's in pain before shaking his head. "I think you can understand why I would avoid going into town as much as I can. I do my shopping early in the morning or late at night. Otherwise, I stick around here."

And to think he had so many dreams. Hobbies, friends, interests. A life. Now his life is bordered by the limits of the trailer park.

"It's been weird," I admit. "Everywhere I go, I'm caught between seeing things as they are now and as they were back then."

"It's like living two different lives. One in the past, one in the present. That's why I'm glad you got out of here. You should be looking ahead, not behind."

But that's the thing. There is no forgetting what's behind me. Not that I ever could have in the first place, but his actions made it practically impossible to move on in a healthy way. I would never lay that burden on him— he's carrying enough of a burden as it is.

But I think he knows. I think he understands.

"How do you keep yourself busy?" I ask, sliding out of my coat and settling back against cushions.

"Oh, you know. I help out around here. Neighbors who need repairs, that sort of thing. I have friends. We visit each other's places and watch TV or play cards. They're good people."

"Of course, you have friends. You always made friends wherever you went."

A shadow passes over his face before he chuckles. "Yes, that served me well for a number of years. Knowing how to make friends and avoid ruffling feathers."

I shudder to think. For so many years, I'd lie in bed at night and stare at the ceiling while imagining him doing the same thing in a far different place. There was a time I was obsessed with prison shows, movies, anything I could get my hands on. I was determined to understand what he must be going through. Finally, Mom told my therapist about it, and he discouraged me from continuing. It was unhealthy.

I understand that now, but back then? It was just another betrayal by my mother. Another way for her to invade my life that didn't involve spending any actual time with me. I understand why, looking back. She was falling apart. She thought she was helping in whatever way she could.

"What about you? How is Boston?" He touches a hand to his chest. "Please, do your old man a favor and tell me you haven't become a Patriots fan."

"How could you even think such a thing?" I laugh as he pretends to wipe sweat from his forehead. "I still bleed green. Besides, the Patriots are nothing without Brady. It's time for the Eagles to step up and take their place as the next dynasty."

"From your lips to Coach Sirianni's ears." He holds up crossed fingers, and I do the same, and we laugh again.

"It's funny. I can't tell you the last time I thought about us watching games together."

Forest of Silence

His smile softens until it's almost sad. "That's funny. I think about it all the time. But then you're a lot busier than I am," he reasons, shrugging it off.

"To tell you the truth, most of the time, one day blends into the next. I have to check my phone to keep it straight."

"Is now the time when I can point out how tired you look? Or will I get my head bit off for it?"

"I won't bite your head off. And I am tired, but that's how it goes."

"You always gave your all to everything," he muses before getting up and crossing the small living room to refill his mug from a pot of coffee that smells slightly burnt, like the carafe has sat on the hot plate for too long. He doesn't seem to mind, drinking it black as he always did.

"You say that like it's a bad thing."

"It's not a good thing when you sacrifice your health for it."

He sounds like Mitch. "I don't think it's going that far just yet."

"I hope it doesn't. You need to take care of yourself, too. You can't give all of you to the rest of the world."

It's the simplest piece of advice, delivered

quietly, with no bells or whistles. No great fanfare. Yet for some reason, his simple words are balm for my soul. All this time, I didn't know I craved advice from my dad.

"Are you hungry?" He turns to the freezer and starts poking around inside. "I haven't got a lot but you're welcome to any of it. Do you still like fish sticks?"

Even if I didn't, I would never say no. "I cannot tell you the last time I had a fish stick."

"I also have those little smiley faced potatoes that you like."

"Smileys? Okay, yeah, let's eat."

He's grinning from ear to ear by the time he leans over to preheat the oven. "Don't worry," he promises with a twinkle in his eye. "I won't overcook them. I know you hate it when they get sunburned."

Chapter 25

Fish sticks and smiley face potato patties. Not exactly gourmet food, but it might be the most delicious meal I've had in as long as I can remember. By the time I put on my coat and give Dad a long, tight hug, it's hard to remember why I was dreading this visit in the first place. I feel lighter and more relaxed than I have in ages. Like his trailer is a gas station and my soul needed to be refilled. I'm all topped off by the time I step out into a night full of flurries. "Here it comes," I murmur, pulling up my hood.

"You be safe out there."

He surprises me by following me down the steps and pulling me in for one more hug. "I guess I'm greedy," he murmurs close to my ear, while I close my eyes and soak in his love. Things will never be the same as they were, but I feel how much he wishes to make things right. And for now, that's enough.

It's not until I'm in the car that I check my phone. It was easy to leave it untouched for hours while we watched the first half of the Thursday night football game. We didn't particularly care about either team, but it didn't matter. The point was spending time together.

My hand trembles when I find an unread text waiting for me. Immediately I dial the field office and leave the phone's speaker on as I pull away from the trailer. "This is Alexis Forrest. I got a message to call in."

"Yes, we've uploaded the data from the Samsung to the shared server. You can use your normal login information to access it."

"Thank you so much." Now, all I have to do is get to the station in one piece, without going twice the speed limit and wrapping my car around a tree. My body is humming, my pulse pounding. What am I going to find? Will it help break the case open, or will it only lead me down yet another dark road?

A dark road like the one I'm traveling down now. I flip on my high beams and ease the pres-

244

sure on the gas pedal once the flurries turn into something a little more substantial. Big, heavy flakes, not the kind that usually fall in the dead of winter when it's so cold, the flakes are tiny, like pellets. It's more like feathers floating down from the sky.

I wish I could shake the image of them landing on Camille's face. If she's still alive out there, is she wondering why no one has come to save her yet? "I'm doing my best," I murmur, leaning over the wheel when my wipers aren't enough to keep the windshield clear from the onslaught coming from the clouds above. A deer darts out of the woods up ahead, and I barely hit the brakes in time to avoid contact. It crosses the road and I wait with my heart pounding until I'm reasonably sure it won't be followed by its friends or family. I won't do Camille any good if I never make it to the station.

But I do make it to the station, where I'm glad to find Andy and his group of goofballs long gone. I'm not as well acquainted with the officers working at this time of night, though no one seems surprised to see me headed back to my makeshift office. The captain is gone for the evening— I'm glad to see it, since he needs to get some rest.

Though he might not be resting for long, depending on what I find here.

It only takes a minute to pull out my laptop and power it up, then to log into the secure server used by the Bureau. My hands are shaking so hard that it takes two tries to type my login and password correctly. I am as full of adrenaline as a rookie on her first day, holding my breath as I navigate the files until I find the folder marked Martin Samsung.

I had a feeling what I would find. An assumption, really, since how many kids have a second, secret phone they go to so much trouble to hide? Such a nice phone, too. I doubt it takes an expert to put two and two together.

Still. There's little satisfaction in being proven right when I pull up a lengthy thread of text messages to and from the same phone number. A number with a local area code. How can I be satisfied or pleased with myself when I am instantly bombarded with photos of a very naked, extremely underage Camille Martin?

"Oh, sweetie," I whisper, wincing as I scroll from one photo to another. There are so many.

The messages themselves are another issue. Their contents. The word explicit doesn't begin

Forest of Silence

to do them justice. Even the ones that are tame by comparison turn my stomach.

Unknown: I love your body.

Unknown: You know what I like. Make me happy, baby.

Unknown: I wish I could touch you right now.

Then there are the messages Camille sent back.

Camille: When I lie in bed, I imagine you here with me.

Camille: I imagine it's your hands touching me.

Camille: I miss you so much.

I have to force myself to scroll all the way back to the beginning, to confirm for myself when it all began. According to the timestamp on the first message Camille sent to her unknown friend, the correspondence began in May. There's nothing saying things didn't start well before then.

This just happens to be the point where evidence started piling up.

Camille was fourteen then— she didn't turn fifteen until summer. A child. And from what I can discern, she wasn't speaking to another child.

KATE GABLE

Camille: I promise, my parents will never find this phone.

Unknown: They better not. You know what would happen.

Camille: I know. They would never understand. They don't get it. They don't get me like you do.

Unknown: That's right. We understand each other. This will be our secret.

If those aren't the words of a groomer, I'll eat my diploma. I might add my badge as dessert.

It wasn't just explicit texts and photos, either.

Unknown: Did you get the money?

Camille: Yes! Thank you so much.

Unknown: I hope you buy something pretty with it.

Camille: Like what?

Unknown: You know what I like. You're always so pretty when you wear pink. And I like seeing you in dresses. Girls your age never wear dresses anymore. But you're so much more mature than they are.

I am officially going to be sick. I never thought I would regret eating fish sticks and

Forest of Silence

smileys, but now they churn in my stomach along with the second Diet Coke I drank.

I know from that last exchange alone this person is an adult. So much more mature than the other kids her age. It's not even original. But then a child wouldn't know that, would they? I can almost see Camille in her room, lying on that neatly made bed, surrounded by her little treasures and books and plants. I can imagine her parents in the same house, grading papers or creating lesson plans, both of them resting easy in the belief they have a daughter who is too smart to get caught up in something like this. I can just imagine how grateful they'd be, seeing for themselves through their students how easy it is for a kid to stumble onto the wrong path. No doubt they considered themselves blessed with a daughter who was too level-headed and conscientious to ever get herself mixed up with a predator.

And all the while he was sending her money in exchange for nude photos.

There's a folder marked *Videos*. I freeze, the cursor hovering over the icon. Do I even want to see this? I have to. Naturally, I'll hand this information over to the captain, and I'm sure we'll look through it together, but something compels me to go through it first on my own. I don't know why. There's no protecting her now. It's too late for that.

I manage to make it roughly thirty seconds into the first video before I have to close it and push away from the desk. The agent in me understands how these things progress. Eventually, photos aren't enough. The predator needs more stimulation. They always have to up the ante. It makes for a more thrilling experience, too. Knowing how dangerous it is.

She never used a name in her messages, and neither did he. It doesn't matter. Deep in my gut I know what I'm going to find when I do a reverse look-up on the phone number she sent messages, photos, and videos to. It feels inevitable.

Somehow, I imagined feeling satisfied, being proven right. There's nothing but emptiness inside when I come up with a name associated with that number. Edward Schiff. "You monster," I whisper, remembering him sitting at his desk. Eating a sandwich from home. Talking about the kids on the debate team and how they wanted to hang out with him. The image of innocence, of concern for the daughter of his coworkers. A kid he taught and coached.

Forest of Silence

And groomed. No way this started in May. You don't start out with nude photos right off the bat. This sort of thing takes time to develop. The man has taught at Broken Hill High for six years. I can't believe he didn't at least meet her before she started attending school there. Faculty picnics, Bring Your Daughter To Work Day. He's known her since she was little.

Somehow, he was able to pay her for nude photos and still chat around the coffeemaker with her parents.

I'm already pulling out my phone, scrolling through to find the captain's contact. "I'm sorry to bother you at home," I tell him, staring at the name on my laptop screen. "But we're going to need to bring Ed Schiff in. Immediately."

As an afterthought, I add, "I hope you haven't eaten lately. Either that, or you'd better have a strong stomach."

Chapter 26

"What is this all about?" Ed Schiff has the audacity to sit with his arms folded, staring straight ahead at the wall opposite his seat in the otherwise empty room. His voice filters through a speaker on my side of the wall separating us. "This is ridiculous. What, do we now invade people's residences without warning in this country? Is this the state of law enforcement nowadays?"

I'm deeply glad for both our sakes to be watching from the other side of the one-way glass looking into the interrogation room. He wouldn't like what I have to say, and I have no business saying it.

But he is certainly testing my self-control.

"I think he's marinated long enough." I

check the time, confirming it's been fifteen minutes since a pair of officers brought him to the station. "Let's see what he has to say."

"Are you good to do this?" Captain Felch is at my side, staring into the room just like I am. It took no time for him to order Schiff be brought in for questioning after he reviewed what I saw. It's no mystery why his voice is so strained.

"I'm good." Every moment I spend watching him become more indignant deepens my resolve. I am very much looking forward to pulling the rug out from under him.

First, I open a bottle of cold water, but a long gulp doesn't do much to cool the heat that's blazed within me ever since I opened that folder and saw everything the forensics team unlocked. But my personal feelings have nothing to do with this, and they won't help Camille. Stay cool. Don't ruin this.

"Oh, I should have known." Schiff throws his hands into the air when I enter the room with folders tucked under my arm. "You know, I've already said everything I have to say to you."

"I spoke with you about your connection to Camille Martin."

"Exactly."

I pause halfway across the room and tip my head to the side. "Did anyone mention her name this evening?"

He swallows hard and sits up a little straighter. "What else would this be about? She's the reason you're here in town, isn't she?"

"Of course. That makes sense." Let him think he's clever. I'm sure that's what appeals to him the most about kids Camille's age. They don't know any better. They look at somebody like him—the cool, understanding teacher—and are drawn like moths to the flame. Finally, an adult who treats them seriously. Finally, somebody who makes them feel heard without talking down to them.

And he takes advantage. Like a spider in the center of the web he's woven, waiting for his innocent prey to become entangled.

"Why am I here, then? I don't have so much as a parking ticket on my record."

"I'm afraid there were a couple of points I was unclear about when it comes to Camille." I sit across from him, placing the folders in front of me but leaving them closed. His narrowed eyes dart in their direction before returning to me. I've piqued his interest.

Forest of Silence

"I told you everything there is to know. These insinuations have already gone too far, and I suggest you hit the brakes before you take things any farther. My lawyer is going to find out about this."

I have no doubt. "It's only a few questions. This doesn't have to take long."

He has the instinct of a predator. I sense the suspicion, the way his mind is turning. Trying to see beneath my bland, flat demeanor. I might be running a few degrees above a simmer inside, but he can't know that.

"Well? What was so crucial that I had to be brought in here when I was about to get ready for bed? You know, I'll have to be in the classroom early in the morning."

He won't be going anywhere near a classroom ever again. "As far as you were aware, was Camille involved with any of the boys on the debate team?"

That's when he makes his first mistake. He scoffs. A simple yes or no would have been a perfectly reasonable answer, the response of an observant but detached third party.

Instead, he revealed his inner thoughts with that simple reaction. "Not likely."

"Oh? That's a pretty definite answer. What makes you think that?"

"She was born old. She's not impressed with boys. She doesn't let herself become distracted by them," he speaks like an authority. Like this is something he's given thought to. How much thought? It makes my skin crawl.

"Yes, I have heard she is a very serious, driven girl who isn't interested in dating." I pause for a beat, then clarify. "Her parents told me that."

Pain pinches his brows together for a second. "They would know."

"Did the two of you ever have a conversation about boyfriends? Anyone at school she might have been getting close to recently? Some things, parents don't know, but a teacher who spends plenty of time with the team he coaches might."

"Are you asking whether we ever had an inappropriate conversation? Because it never happened. There's a line."

"We can agree on that."

My gaze remains focused on him as I nudge the top folder away from the one beneath it, then slide it his way. The contents are the same as what's still in front of me.

"Would you care to explain what you'll find in that folder?"

"What's inside?"

"Please, take a look. I printed two copies so we can go through them together."

He lifts the cover slowly, like he expects a spider to jump out. He'll wish it was something as harmless as a spider. When he first sets eyes on the text thread, his face goes a ghostly shade of white, and his mouth falls open before snapping shut. "What is this?" he finally croaks.

"Print outs from the very lengthy text conversation that took place between Camille Martin on a second, hidden cell phone, and the individual to whom this second phone number is registered. Does that number look familiar to you, Mr. Schiff?"

"I—"

"And this second phone. Would you care to take a guess as to the account the phone is linked to? Can you guess who pays the bill?"

"W-wait a minute."

"Tell me."

Sweat beads on his upper lip and begins rolling down his temples. "It's mine. I bought the phone. That's my number."

"So am I correct in assuming that since the

number is yours, you were the individual who exchanged these texts? You are the person talking to Camille?"

He wants to deny it. I see it in his ticking jaw, his shifting eyes, the way his breathing gets faster. He's an animal in a trap. "I … I only texted her."

"Where is Camille?"

"I don't know!" he shouts, spittle flying from his mouth. "I don't have the first idea."

"Then let's talk about something you know more about." I tap the printout with two fingers. "When did this start? The texts go back to May. Was that the first time the two of you ever spoke this way?"

"I … don't remember, exactly …" His tongue darts over his lips while he rubs the back of his neck. "I can't say."

"What did you do with her?"

"Nothing! I'm telling you, I don't know where she is."

"Where were you the night she disappeared, Mr. Schiff?"

"I was home, I was grading papers, I swear."

"And if we were to go to your home now? What would we find?"

"She's not there! I'm telling you, I have no idea where she is. I had nothing to do with this."

"So this is where you drew the line? This was it?"

"Yes, yes!"

"Because we managed to find everything that was on this phone. Keep that in mind before you say another word."

"This was it. The texts, the photos, all of that. I never touched her."

"Do you want me to read some of these texts where you both imply very heavily that you've put your hands on her?"

"That was all made up. Fantasy stuff."

"Eventually, fantasy wasn't enough."

"That's not how it was, I'm telling you." He pounds his fist on the table before holding his head in his hands. "I didn't hurt her. I don't know where she is."

"Have you ever taught at Hawthorne Academy, Mr. Schiff?"

The question startles him into lifting his head. "What? No."

"Have you ever been acquainted with any of the students there?"

"You're talking about that dead girl from the

private school. Right? Do you think I had something to do with that?"

"I'm only asking questions, sir."

"I've never worked there, and anybody there can tell you that. And I didn't know that girl. I don't know any of those kids. Why would I? Do you think I go around actively looking for kids to befriend?"

"You said it yourself. When we first met, remember? Plenty of kids have jobs in town. Was Camille's the only one you paid visits to? Are there other phones in your name, Mr. Schiff?"

The door opens, and the sound of it snaps me out of whatever had me in its grips. "Agent Forrest?" It's Felch, and he sounds stern.

"I want my lawyer." Schiff sinks back into his chair. His head drops back until he's staring at the ceiling tiles. "I'm not saying another word without my lawyer."

"That's fine, sir. We'll arrange that for you. You sit tight." The captain then jerks his head toward the hall and I take the hint, stepping out of the room. As soon as the door's closed, I turn on my heel and prepare to defend myself.

"Relax." He holds up his hands, shaking his head. "I'm not trying to chew you out, even if you started going a little too far. You needed to back off and breathe."

He isn't wrong, though he did provide the break Schiff needed to come to his senses and demand his lawyer. He might not have done that if we hadn't been interrupted.

And I might have ruined everything by calling him a filthy pedophile if the captain hadn't stopped me.

Chapter 27

"He'll be charged tomorrow, first thing." The captain checks his watch and frowns. "I'm not sure if it's worth going home and going to bed at this point."

"I'm sorry I didn't wait until morning to reach out."

All that earns me is a roll of his eyes. "That is not the sort of evidence you wait to share. Especially when there's still a girl missing."

"A girl he kidnapped."

"We still have no proof of that."

"We both know he did it."

"Easy, now."

I have to grit my teeth, he sounds much too patronizing right now. I know he means well, but it isn't easy to swallow my pride and accept being chastised. Even when it's offered gently.

"I know it looks that way," he continues in a slow, measured cadence I'm sure is supposed to calm me down. "He is most certainly a prime suspect, about that, there is no argument. But we can't go around throwing accusations without proof, and we have none."

"Yet."

"Yet. But you and I both know that's a very big three-letter word. If and when evidence is found connecting him to Camille's disappearance, that'll be a different story. Right now, we only have him on solicitation and possession of child pornography."

It's good to know he'll be spending the night in jail, and many nights after this one, but it isn't enough. Like settling for an appetizer when I want the full meal. Strangely enough, that's sort of how it feels. I'm hungry to see this man brought to justice for what he's done. For all of it. "We have to get a warrant to search the house."

"It's already been done." When my eyes go wide, he shakes his head, snickering. "What, you think we're so backwards here in Broken Hill, we don't know how to get things done? We arranged for that while you were questioning Schiff. The judge signed off faster than I've ever seen."

"That's great news."

"And in the morning, we'll send a few officers over there with you and you can pick the place apart."

I'm glad to have the go ahead, but I'm not completely satisfied. He must see it in my face. I try not to let my feelings show, but sometimes I'm not successful. He scowls after studying my expression. "What? What's the problem now?"

I fix my face before shaking my head. "There's no problem." It's not easy, lying so casually.

"Concern? Is that a better word?"

He's already seen through me. What's the use of giving him the whole song and dance? "I would like to go straight over there, of course. I don't want to wait."

"I'm not surprised." He rubs his eyes with a tired groan before dropping his hands to his sides. "No one respects your dedication to this case more than I do. I mean that wholeheartedly. But you won't do Camille any favors if you wear yourself down. You need to sleep."

It's barely past midnight. "It isn't that late.

And I won't get a wink unless I've already been through the house."

"Do you mean you'll lie in bed like a kid on Christmas Eve, counting down the minutes?"

"Not exactly, but close." I appreciate him trying to keep things light, to I make sure I'm not too completely absorbed in the case. I'm sure he's seen examples of cops who lose their sense of perspective. I have, too. And I have my psychology background. I know how easy it is for the mind to become warped, even when a person has the best intentions.

That is not what's happening now. It's been too long, and Camille is still out there some-where, and this is our only shot so far of tracking her down. "If I were kidnapped and kept away from my family, I don't know if I would care very much whether the people looking for me were sleepy. I would want them to find me."

His already solemn expression sags a little, deepening the brackets around his mouth. "I understand that."

"And for all we know, he could've been connected to Lila somehow. It could have been him she was planning to meet that night."

"Could be."

"For all we know, he could have another phone somewhere. Something that belongs to her. Anything."

"You're still of the opinion the two cases are linked?"

This is tough. I can tell from the way he asks he's not so sure, and I can understand that. "Let me put it this way. How many missing girls have there been in Broken Hill over the past, I don't know, twenty or thirty years?"

"I haven't been here that long, but then you know that." He releases a deep sigh, while his brows draw together in concern. "Aside from the typical runaways, who we quickly find, there haven't been many."

"Exactly. Yes, there are always kids running away, getting into trouble, what have you. But kidnappings? Murders? Considering there hasn't been a case like this in Broken Hill since my sister's, I think it's a pretty big coincidence for two girls to disappear within days of each other, and one of them to end up dead. If it's not Ed Schiff connecting them, it's someone else. I'm willing to admit I was wrong if he's not our guy, but if we're going to eliminate him, we need to do it now."

"Danny Clifton did date both girls."

"Yes, but Danny Clifton was out of town when Camille disappeared," I remind him. "And he was home studying when Lila was making her escape from Hawthorne. And I'm still convinced he was genuinely distraught when I broke the news. He really cared about her."

Something happening outside the captain's office draws our attention. He stands and joins me at the window in time to watch a pair of officers lead Ed Schiff away from booking.

What a difference an hour can make. When I first saw him in the interrogation room, he was the picture of icy anger and self-righteousness. He must really have believed there was no way for anyone to access that data. It never occurred to him that might be why we brought him in.

And I suppose he figured the assertion that he never laid a hand on her would make a difference. As if what he already did wasn't bad enough.

The broken, weeping man led past the window could not be more different from the confident, self-assured teacher I met before. Amazing how little it takes to bring someone like that to their knees.

There's no real satisfaction in watching him crumble. Not the way I expected. Mostly, I'm sad. That girl lost some of her innocence thanks to him. Even if he has nothing to do with what she's going through now, he left his mark on her life. "She did tell Danny she wanted someone more mature," I whisper, finally putting it together. Hindsight has a way of making everything seem so obvious. "She was thinking about him."

"And that's why she broke it off with Danny."

"It adds up." Even if I can't imagine dumping the hockey star for a middle-aged teacher but then teenagers have a way of acting against their best interests. "Well, now we have an idea of how long this was really going on."

"To think." He turns toward me looking sorrowful. "Tess and Brian. This was going on right under their noses all this time."

"I'm sure if you asked them, they would've told you they trust him." And now the burning determination to find Camille and bring her home is stronger than ever. "We can't let them face that and face losing their daughter."

"Why do I think you're about to tell me you're going to Ed Schiff's house tonight?"

"Because that's exactly what I'm going to do."

"At least let me call Andy to go in with you."

The image of a pin popping a balloon fills my mind. "Andy? Andy Cobb?"

"I know, he's a little much sometimes," he tells me as he goes to his desk and picks up the phone. "But he is a good cop. He takes his work seriously, which is probably why he's made it his mission to make you feel uncomfortable. He wanted this case for himself."

"So long as he agrees to stay out of my way."

"That, I can't guarantee."

Me and Andy Cobb searching a house together in the middle of the night. The idea is almost enough to make me reconsider waiting until morning, since I'll need to be on top of my game if there's any hope of not strangling him.

Chapter 28

"Remind me why we can't do this in the morning." Andy Cobb greets me with his usual charming attitude the moment I step out of my car in front of Ed Schiff's house. He's already parked in the driveway, leaning against his car, holding a steaming cup between gloved hands.

"Sorry to disturb your beauty sleep," I tell him as I approach, "but if you saw what I saw tonight, you'd want to tear this guy's house apart to make sure he wasn't stalking other little girls. At the very least, you'd lose sleep over it."

"You know, my little brother had him for social studies in his senior year." He barely stifles a yawn, and I notice now that he's in a pair of faded sweatpants, with an old University of Maine sweatshirt peeking out from under his coat. "I think that's the first year Schiff taught at the school. Luke always said he sort of came off like a creep."

"Really?" That sort of thing is easy to say now that we both know beyond the shadow of a doubt the man is a creep … putting it mildly.

"Yeah, said he was always a little too interested in the kids' lives. Asking what they did that weekend, if they had any plans coming up, stuff like that." He shrugs as we approach the front door, where a uniformed officer waits. They cleared the scene, making sure Camille wasn't locked somewhere on the premises before we arrived.

"Sometimes, awkward people are just awkward people," he concludes with a sigh. "And sometimes, they're exactly as bad as you thought they were."

I wonder if he knows how different he is when he's not performing for an audience. When it's just the two of us, he's a bit chattier than I prefer, but there's none of the sense of him having something personal against me.

"Where do you want to start?" Yes, he even asks for my opinion instead of shoving his way past me and strutting into the house. It's almost

271

enough to make me ask what he did with the real Andy Cobb.

"His bedroom seems the most logical place." He nods and follows me up the stairs of the small, saltbox style home. The first thing I notice is how neat it is. Extremely tidy. There are even lines in the carpet from the vacuum cleaner, all perfectly straight like he deliberately, carefully placed them. Not the sort of thing you arrest a man over, but certainly interesting. I'm building a profile for him ... at least in my mind — and the fact that he's so deliberate and fastidious in this area of his life makes me wonder why he would make such a sloppy mistake as the one he made with Camille.

"Do you have any idea what we might be looking for?" Andy asks as we walk down a narrow hall. The stairs take a ninety-degree turn toward the top. To my right is a spare bedroom he apparently uses as his office. To my left, a bathroom, and beyond that the master bedroom. There's a third, small bedroom at the end of the short hallway, and it's made up like a guest room.

"I'm not sure," I admit, pulling on my gloves while standing in the doorway to the master bedroom. "I only know there's got to be something. I'll know it when I see it. Another phone, maybe. Clothes, maybe a token, like panties. Pictures. Anything that doesn't seem like it belongs in the home of a single schoolteacher who lives alone."

"Got it." To my surprise, he takes the home office without any further comment, while I begin looking through drawers in the bedroom.

Something that strikes me right away, the way he arranges his clothes in the dresser drawers. They remind me of Camille's very careful folding and arranging. Who taught whom this trick? Was Camille trying to model herself after her very mature, disciplined boyfriend? I hope that's not what it is. I hate to imagine her being so wrapped up in him.

I know very well how easy it is for a teenage girl to become wrapped up. And that's what makes my heart sink. This poor, deluded kid.

Even though my skin is crawling ever so slightly, there's nothing in any of the drawers beyond what I would expect to find. No false bottoms, nothing taped underneath them. I give his nightstand the same treatment and come up with nothing noteworthy before turning my attention to the closet.

"How's it going in there?" I call out across the hall to Andy.

"I would like to bleach my brain as soon as possible. If that's alright with you."

Naturally, curiosity leads me across the hall to where he is using the tip of a pen to go through hanging file folders lined up in the desk drawer.

"What is that?" I ask as I approach.

He responds by using his gloved fingers to hold one of the hanging folders open wide enough for me to see what Ed was storing there. "Oh, you must be kidding me," I whisper in disgust.

"I wish I was."

The man has been compiling his own personal database of images from magazines. Teen magazines, from the looks of it. Models in bathing suits. Girls in dresses, workout gear, even pajamas.

"What a creep." He goes to another folder and we both groan at what are clearly printout images from the school's website. Girls in field hockey skirts, the school's swim team in their bathing suits. "He's had his eyes on a lot of the girls," I muse while my stomach turns.

"And when I think of this guy spending so

much time around these kids." He growls before turning away from the drawer. "It's disgusting."

It is, and now I'm more convinced than ever. "Camille can't be the only one he ever tried this with," I decide on my way across the hall. "No chance. Not after he took all the time to compile this. Eventually, looking and imagining isn't enough."

"You aren't telling me anything I don't already know, Agent Forrest."

"I wasn't— never mind."

"No, what were you going to say?"

I close my eyes in front of the open closet and count slowly to five before daring to answer. "I was going to say I wasn't trying to share a lesson. I was thinking out loud. I'm sorry if that offended you."

"I didn't say I was offended."

"Then what is it?" I return to the doorway and stare into the office. "Why do you make it your personal mission to single me out whenever possible? Why do you take it so personally that I'm here?"

"I don't know what you're talking about." He pulls the folders and sets them on the desk. "I think we should take these in. Maybe we can identify some of these girls, if they're still at the school. We could ask if he ever pulled anything with them."

It's not a bad idea, though I can't imagine spending all that time when it might lead nowhere. I decide to keep my concerns to myself. If he wants to dig into it, let him. Let him feel like he's accomplishing something. He'll be less likely to get in my way.

I return to the bedroom closet, which is just as fastidiously organized as everything else. The more I search, the more frustrated I become. This isn't helping. None of this is helping.

"You should see this bathroom," Andy calls out from the room next door. There's a door connecting the two rooms and I open it to find him going through the medicine cabinet. "Nothing here any stronger than aspirin." He sounds disappointed.

"What were you hoping for? Roofies?"

Our eyes meet in the mirrored cabinet door when he closes it. "Is it too much to ask for a break in this case?"

"I know what you mean." I take in the extraordinarily clean room, then sniff the air. "Bleach."

He opens the door to the vanity, where cleaning products are lined up in pretty little

Forest of Silence

rows. "There was no evidence of cleaning fluids on the body, was there?"

He's talking about Lila. "No. The body was left as-is."

"Does it strike you that someone with a cleaning fetish would make it a point to clean any evidence of themselves off a dead body?"

I see what he means. It doesn't add up. If Ed Schiff's predilections developed into obsession until he couldn't settle for photos and videos anymore, his natural compulsion to make sure everything is clean and organized wouldn't let him take a chance of leaving evidence behind. His DNA, carpet fibers from around the house. He would want to be sure she was completely free of anything that could link him to her.

"I'm not giving up."

"Nobody said you had to. I was only making a point." He finishes inspecting the room, then shrugs. "Listen. This guy makes me sick. People like him make me sick in general. But let's face it. So far, we haven't had anything to hint to either of those girls ever being here. Any girls at all. He's a pig, and he's going to prison, but that doesn't make him a murderer."

"I know." I pinch the bridge of my nose, aware of the headache threatening to announce itself. "But I can't give up until we've searched this whole house. If you don't feel like it, that's fine, but I have to."

"Nice try, Agent Forrest." He follows me to the spare bedroom which we quickly check together. There's nothing more than a made-up bed and an empty nightstand in here. The closet is free of anything but bare hangers. And as is the case with the rest of the house, everything is perfectly neat. Even when there's nobody sleeping in here.

"Nice try, what?"

"Chain of custody. We find something around here, we don't want to let him slip through our fingers because I wasn't here to corroborate the discovery."

As it turns out, there is no evidence. No extra phone. No trophies— clothes, jewelry, anything of the sort. Aside from the images he keeps in his desk drawer, there's nothing around here to indicate he's more than a pedophile.

It's nearly three in the morning by the time we leave, no closer to finding Camille than we were when we started. Andy is smart enough to say good night without making any further comments beyond a quick, "See you later."

Forest of Silence

"Yeah. And thanks for coming out at this time of night."

"No need to thank me." He opens his car door and slides behind the wheel. "I didn't do it for you."

No, he didn't, and I need to stop taking this case as personally as I do. It's darn near impossible, though. I set out to find this girl, and I haven't managed it yet. I've never been someone who takes failure well. This is no exception.

Once I'm behind the wheel, alone, I let my weary head touch the back of the seat before releasing a sad sigh. "I'm sorry, kid," I whisper, closing my eyes and swallowing back the emotion that's suddenly clogging my throat. I'm doing my best.

Sadly, my best isn't good enough. I'm starting to wonder whether I'll ever find who took Camille and what they did with her.

At least, not before it's too late to do anything about it.

Chapter 29

This would be the perfect day to pull the blankets over my head and pretend the rest of the world doesn't exist. The light coming in between the slats in the blinds is thin and gray, and there's a chill in the air that seems to have seeped into my bones while I was sleeping. Surprisingly enough, I was able to drop off quickly after peeling off my clothes and falling into bed without even washing my face. I draw the blankets a little closer to my chin and squeeze my eyes shut like that will buy me a little more time to lie around and feel sorry for myself.

But that didn't work when I was a kid trying to avoid going to school, and it's not going to work now. There's a lot more on the line than a

Forest of Silence

potential pop quiz or having to face my boyfriend after we got in a little fight. Still, my body curls into a ball and I shiver, and not entirely thanks to the chill.

Where is Camille? If Schiff didn't take her, who did?

I pry one eye open, staring dolefully at my cell on the nightstand. It buzzed at some point close to dawn, but I was in no condition to do more than roll over and go back to sleep. Now I reach out and snatch it, pulling it under the blanket before I let out any of the body heat I've managed to capture. Mom can do all the renovations she wants to this rambling old place, but there are too many little cracks and crevices for the cold air to leak through.

There's a text from one of my contacts at the field office. Schiff's phone data confirms Camille Martin was the only person he was texting.

I have no doubt they were as thorough as can be. It's what they do. Meaning I'm at a dead end when it comes to Lila, and since no one has reached out with any news to the contrary, Schiff has not broken down and confessed to kidnapping Camille.

In other words, I'm back at square one.

And I am less certain than ever that Ed Schiff had anything to do with Camille's disappearance.

I could move in one of two directions now. I could double down and dig deeper into Ed, scrambling desperately to make a connection that might not exist. Or I can move on, start again, ask questions and dig deeper. Dig deeper into what? I don't know. Yes, the discovery of Camille's relationship with her teacher is explosive and would be a major story in and of itself were there not a disappearance involved. But there is a disappearance involved, and it could be much worse than a disappearance, but so far the relationship is the only secret I've managed to uncover. That was supposed to be the smoking gun. That was supposed to be the big breakthrough.

I can't lie in bed all day, as much as I want to. When I arrived at the house, I found a note from Mom on my pillow saying she had to meet with prospective sellers on the other side of town first thing in the morning. At least I don't feel like I have to tiptoe around and avoid her for the sake of avoiding uncomfortable questions I can't answer. Questions that are only uncomfortable because I don't want to admit how lost I am. How discouraged.

A hot shower goes a long way toward thawing the ice in my veins, and by the time I pull on a thick sweater and heavy leggings, I feel almost human. The forecast called for snow throughout the night, so it's no surprise when I finally pull up the blinds and find a blanket of snow covering the garden beyond the bedroom window. The streets have been plowed and treated − if there's one thing they're careful about around here, it's cleaning up after snow. Tourists can't meander around town and enjoy the idyllic, snow-kissed New England vibe if the streets are impassable and the sidewalks too dangerous to walk.

Rather than stick around to fix myself breakfast, I venture a trip outside with the aid of heavy boots that help me navigate the wet and somewhat icy driveway. It looks like Mom already spread salt before heading out, but I add more, then drive down to Main Street. I can't bring myself to go to the station, at least not right away. Not right now. I need a little more time between run-ins with Andy, for one thing. For another, I'm too heartsick to hide it from the overly interested gazes of the people there.

I'm already parking the car in an open space and headed for the bookstore before I quite know I've made up my mind to do it. Mitch is there. Mitch always knows how to make things better, even if all he does is listen. And that's what I need more than anything, except a new lead in the case. Somebody to listen, somebody who understands me.

My heart swells at his transformative smile when he looks up and finds me waiting in line for coffee. The people waiting in front of me make polite conversation and talk about last night's football game. It's a warm, friendly atmosphere. Mitch greets everybody by name and knows their order before they have to open their mouth. This is exactly the kind of place I would have imagined him owning even if I never set eyes on it. He's always known just how to make people feel at ease and appreciated. Too many business owners don't understand the value of making their customers feel like more than walking wallets.

"I have to admit, I don't know your order yet." He places his hands on the counter and gives me another one of his deadly grins. I swear, he has the power to make my heart stop.

"Something nice, and strong, and hot, please."

"How about a large latte with an extra shot of espresso and cinnamon on the foam?"

"It sounds heavenly." He ignores the money I try to hand over in favor of turning away and fixing the drink, so I tuck the cash into the tip jar. Once the drink is ready, he brings it over to one of the tables and takes a seat.

"It'll be quiet for a while now," he predicts. Sure enough, I was the last person in line. It's past nine o'clock now, so I imagine a lot of people are at work by this time.

"I didn't come here for a free drink, you know." A drink that's so delicious, I can't help but moan softly when the milky, cinnamon-spiked coffee touches my tongue.

"I know. But whenever somebody comes in looking as beat up as you do, I try to take care of them."

"By telling them they look beat up? My, you're such a gentleman." I can tease him, but my heart's not in it.

And he sees that, because he's always been able to see through me. "I take it things aren't going so well."

"You are correct."

"I'm sorry. I wish there were something I could do. You have no idea how much I wish I could help."

"I know." I hold the paper cup between my hands, grateful for the warmth even though the store is nice and toasty thanks to a merry little fire crackling in the hearth near the front window. "I just can't shake the feeling that I'm letting everybody down."

"You aren't."

"Easy for you to say."

"Because it's true. You can't fix the entire world, Alexis. Sometimes terrible things happen, and we wish with all our might we could fix it." Pain passes over his face and I know he's talking about himself. How he wishes he had driven Camille home.

"You could stand to take a little of your own advice."

"We're talking about you now, not me."

"Convenient." I take another sip of my coffee before shaking my head. "There has to be something I've missed. There must be. We know now that Ed Schiff was having an inappropriate relationship with her— that's off the record," I whisper, horrified at myself for letting it slip. "I'm sure it will come out soon enough. By the end of the day, at the latest. He'll be formally charged this morning."

He looks shaken, but his shock soon turns grim. "Well, at the very least, you helped put an end to that. He could easily have moved on to another girl."

That still doesn't help. Yes, it's good to know the man won't be menacing anyone else, but it doesn't bring Camille home to the people who love her. "I've got to do something else. There's pressure on my chest like an elephant sitting on it. I hear a clock ticking in my head all the time."

"You have to take care of yourself."

"I have to take care of Camille."

"Fine. Be stubborn." He stands when a younger couple enters the store and makes their way back to where we're sitting. "But I hope you expect to have me checking in on you nonstop. Somebody has to make sure you're taking care of yourself." I frown and narrow my eyes, but inside it's another story. My heart swells and my pulse picks up speed and once he's turned around, I can grin to myself before getting up and heading to the door. He cares. I can't help but feel touched. Flattered. Wanted.

That can wait. What am I doing, sitting here feeling sorry for myself? Must be more I can do.

Think, think. There are avenues I have yet to explore. Schiff said he never worked at the boarding school. I think I'm going to confirm that for myself rather than take his word for it. I can't afford to leave any stone unturned.

And what if it gets you nowhere? The voice of doubt, right on schedule. The fact is, I don't know what I'll do next if it gets me nowhere. Sometimes, building a case is like climbing a staircase while it's in the process of being constructed. There's no looking past the next step, because there is no next step after that. I have to build it as I go and keep climbing. Frustrating, but that's reality.

Right now, I don't even have enough materials to build the next step. It's sheer faith that gets me in the car and rolling away from the bookstore.

Faith that's becoming thinner every day.

Chapter 30

As I drive, I leave a voice memo for myself, letting my stream of consciousness lead the way. Sometimes, a brain dump helps shake free something I forgot or a hole in an alibi I didn't catch the first time around.

"Somebody picked Camille up between the bookstore and her house," I muse while carefully navigating streets that might be free of snow but in some places still feature icy patches of slush that didn't quite get picked up by the plows and have now been run over so many times they're slick as glass.

"We know Danny Clifton was out of town at a game with plenty of witnesses to corroborate," I continue. "We cannot confirm where Ed Schiff was that night. He claims he was home grading papers, but of course, there's no way to prove he was home all night without any footage from the neighbors— check with them just in case. I might be able to prove he left the house, thus poking a hole in his story. But so what if there isn't footage of him bringing Camille back to the house?"

I take a deep breath to ward off the panic creeping into my voice. "There was nothing in his home to point to Camille ever stepping foot inside. No trophies, no mementos. Could the relationship really have gone no further than a bunch of texts, photos, and videos? Is it worth questioning the girls in his class and on the debate team, just in case?" That might be worth pursuing, come to think of it. Once word gets out of his being charged, there might be more kids ready to come forward and describe their interactions. The teachers might be willing to speak, as well, once they get over the surprise.

If they are surprised.

There's a definite possibility that they won't be. Sometimes, people like Ed think they have everybody fooled. There always seems to be at least one eagle-eyed witness who sees through the façade. I'll run that by the captain first, but it might be a pretty good idea. If he were ever overly friendly with one of the other girls, they might be able to tell me about … Something. Something I can use.

It sounds like there's a rabid animal in the car with me, but that's just my angry, helpless growl.

"Check with the captain about reaching out to Lila's parents," I continue. "There could be a secret relationship we aren't aware of. If Camille was careful enough that her parents never caught on, and it took me pulling her room apart after it had already been explored to find what she was hiding, who is to say Lila wasn't just as good at hiding things? Her roommates had no idea she was planning to run away. What else was she lying about?"

But is there any hope of me ever finding anything else? I don't know. I really don't. Not when I've already been forbidden to speak with the students. I can't even guarantee I'll be allowed on campus once I pull up to the guard house. It will take a lot of fast talking— and, of course, my badge. I hate to throw my weight around, but there is such a thing as impeding an ongoing investigation. I would like to watch President Winters' reaction if I were to inform him of this. It might be worth a laugh, especially since he's been less than cordial more than once.

I try not to take things personally, but there are some things I can't dismiss so easily.

Once I've left the downtown area, the street widens into a two-lane road. Conditions out here require me to slow down quite a bit and pay closer attention. There's a solid mile or two of woods to pass through before reaching campus, and many of the branches crisscrossing over the road hang lower than usual thanks to the snow and ice weighing them down. It would be magical if it weren't so treacherous. I'm thankful for the lack of traffic—yet another positive about getting out of bed later than I normally would.

There's a lump on the side of the road coming up on my right. A large, misshapen lump that I first assume is an animal that was struck at some point. I slow the car further until I'm practically crawling, just in case there's still life left in it and it decides to lurch into my path.

It doesn't. And on closer inspection, what I originally assumed was black fur looks more like… a blanket.

I barely take time to pull over a few dozen feet from the lump before parking the car. I don't know what it is. Instinct, maybe? Desperation? If it had been a trash bag, I would have kept moving. It was definitely a blanket back there, and it was definitely covering something.

And when I step out of the car and turn around, my new angle gives me the benefit of seeing what wasn't visible as I approached; hair. Dark hair.

My boots make it easier to scramble over the ice and snow built up on the shoulder of the road after the plows passed through. The only thing I hear is the heavy thud of my heart and the blood rushing in my ears. I barely take time to pull out a pair of gloves before pulling back one corner of the blanket, holding my breath, with dread and hope fighting for control.

"Oh, no." I barely hear my own voice. She's as white as the snow around her, making her dark locks and brows stand out midnight black in comparison. There's a bruise along her left cheek bone, and her bottom lip is split, the blood crusted. Scratches along her right cheek and a cut above her right eyebrow.

But it's her.

"Camille!" I might be screaming it, I don't know. I hardly hear myself over the roar in my ears. "Camille, wake up. Talk to me. Camille!"

No, not like this. Please, not like this. I touch my ear to her chest while pressing two fingers against her neck — the faint pulse tears a sob from me. She's alive. Barely.

"Come on, sweetheart. Stay with me." My hands are shaking as I pull away the sodden, half-frozen blanket. It's not doing her any good, anyway. At a time like this, there's concern over contaminating evidence, but what matters most is getting her warm. I pull my phone from my pocket before removing my coat and wrapping it around her thin, frozen body. She's dressed the way she was the night she vanished, except for the absence of her coat and backpack.

As soon as I get an answer at the station, I bark out, "I found Camille Martin! She's on Route One, between downtown and Hawthorne Academy." I look around, searching for a mile marker or some landmark to identify, but quickly give up. "You'll see my car on the side of the road. Hurry, she's practically frozen to death!"

"But she's alive?"

"I have a weak pulse, yes. Hurry, we've got to get her to a hospital. We'll also need a team out here to work the scene." Once I have their confirmation, I run back to my car, where my

Forest of Silence

emergency kit waits in the trunk. You don't grow up in Maine and make your home in Boston unless you're prepared for a surprise winter storm that might get you stranded somewhere. There are two heavy blankets in there, which I grab and take back to Camille, wrapping them around her limp body.

"You're safe now." I'm not sure if she hears me, but just in case she does. "You're safe. I have you. We're going to get you to the hospital, we're going to call your parents, and everything is going to be alright now. You're safe now. You have to stay with me, okay? Stay with me, Camille."

The approaching sirens are the sweetest sound I've heard lately, and I wave my arms overhead once the flashing lights are visible. I don't know when I started crying, but it's not long before the lights blur thanks to my tears.

Chapter 31

"Alexis." I barely have time to register the sound of my own name being called out before I am almost tackled to the floor by the Martins, who instantly sandwich me in a bear hug. Tess weeps softly, and I notice Brian shaking, too, holding back his own emotion as he hugs me from behind one day after his daughter's discovery.

"Thank you, thank you, thank you." They are both teary-eyed but smiling once they release me so I can breathe.

"Anybody else would have driven right by her," Tess reminds me as she wipes her cheeks. "But you didn't. You stopped."

"The doctor said she might have frozen to death given a little more time." Brian wraps his arms around his wife, who buries her face in his chest. "You saved her. You saved our little girl."

"I'm just glad I happened to be on my way past her at the time." The door to her room is open, but all I can see from here is the foot of her bed. "How is she? I got the call she was awake, but wanted to give you a little time to spend with her before I came in."

"She's exhausted, still a little dazed— she was extremely dehydrated and malnourished when she came in, but now that she's had saline and nutrients through her IV, she is coherent and alive. She's alive." Brian claps a hand over his mouth to stifle a laugh that sounds tinged with disbelief. "I'm sorry. What a strange reaction to have."

"It's not strange," I assure him. "You're going through a whole roller coaster right now."

"We wanted to believe, of course we did," Tess whispers. "But there's always that part of you …"

"I understand." After all, I was losing my faith. When you're aware of the statistics, of how unlikely it is to find a victim after a few days, that knowledge is always with you. You can hope all you want, but part of you has to be realistic, as well.

"Would it be alright if I went in and spoke with her now?" I ask. I'm champing at the bit but aware of their privacy, too. "I won't keep her long. I don't want to exhaust her any further. But …"

"Of course, you have a job to do." Suddenly Tess wraps me in another tight hug. "And thank you for finding out about that monster. Thank you for stopping him."

"I can't believe we worked alongside that pig for so long and we didn't have a clue." Brian shakes his head mournfully. "I shudder to think how many other girls …"

"Believe me, we'll find out all about that now that he's behind bars and awaiting trial. I'm just glad we were able to get to the bottom of it all."

The Martins suggest going to the cafeteria for something to eat, giving me time to speak to Camille alone once they've introduced me to their daughter. Tess takes my hand and pulls me along with her. "Sweetheart, this is Agent Forrest. She found you on the road. She was investigating your disappearance."

As an afterthought, Tess adds, "I had her as a student at Broken Hill. I'd like to take all the credit for how exceptional she is, obviously."

Forest of Silence

Camille sits partly upright in the bed, in a room chock-full of flowers and balloons and stuffed animals. Word spreads fast around here. Especially when it comes to a missing girl miraculously found alive.

"Thank you," her voice is soft, sweet. "Thank you so much for finding me. I didn't think anybody would, but I was so tired, and I didn't know where I was, and it was snowing and I couldn't see—"

"It's okay now." Her heart monitor beeps faster with every word as her panic grows. "You're safe now. And no matter what we talk about here, I need you to remember you're safe. Can you do that for me?"

Her head bobs up and down, but her wide eyes immediately seek out her mother.

Brian clears his throat. "I can go down to the cafeteria on my own and bring something back," he suggests. Not a bad idea. She doesn't seem to be in a good place, not that I would expect her to be. She'll want her mother here with her as she relives the most horrific experience of her young life.

I'm as gentle as I can be, taking the spare chair that's positioned at Camille's right side. "If you don't mind, I'm going to record our conversation so I don't miss anything later on. We're still actively investigating your case. We want to find this person. But only if it's okay with you to be recorded."

"Sure, that's fine."

Once I've started a new file and established the date and time, I place the phone on a wheeled table that sits across Camille's lap and holds a Styrofoam cup of juice and a box of tissues. "Camille. Can you describe for me what happened the night you were taken? I understand you left your job and were going to walk home."

She licks her chapped lips before nodding. "Yeah, I was on the way home. It was cold, and I was walking fast. I had my earbuds in. I didn't hear the car until it was next to me."

I hear the self-reproach in her voice. No doubt she's blamed herself countless times the way Mitch has blamed himself. "It's alright. These things happen, and it wasn't your fault. Can you describe the car?"

Her forehead creases in concentration, but she shakes her head away. "I swear, I've tried so many times to remember what it looked like. But everything happened so fast. It was dark blue, but I can't remember what kind of car it was or anything like that."

"What do you remember happening once the car stopped?"

"All of a sudden, there was something over my mouth in my nose. Like a cloth. And something that smelled sweet."

Chloroform. I would bet my life on it.

"And then all of a sudden, everything went dark. I… I don't remember anything between then and when I woke up."

"And what did happen when you woke up? Can you describe where you were?"

At first, but I'm afraid I've already pushed too hard. Her chin quivers, and Tess sits on the bed, taking Camille's hand. When her hospital bracelet slides further down her arm, I notice the chafing on her wrist. "Remember what the agent said, honey. You're safe now. All of that is in the past. He can't hurt you now."

Camille exhales. "It was like a cabin."

"Can you describe it?"

"It was like… The walls were all wood. Like boards, you know? I was in a little room with a window, but it was all dirty and I couldn't see out of it. I could hear animals out there, so I figured I was in the woods."

"That's great. That's a great start."

My approval seems to loosen her up, and now the words are flowing. "I was on, like, a metal bed with a thin mattress. I could feel the springs almost poking through it, and it was dirty, and it smelled. It was cold in there. There was one of those, you know, old metal stoves in the corner. But it didn't get used. But there were lots of blankets. They were gross, but they were warm."

"Was there anybody else there? Did you hear anyone else?"

"Not until he came in." Her chin quivers again. "And it was really dark. There was no light in the room, but he was carrying a lantern, that kind of thing. Only I still couldn't see his face really well. He wore a hat."

"Like a knit hat?"

"No, like a baseball cap. So there was just a shadow over his face."

"I see. Can you give me a description of him?"

"I… I don't know…" She's starting to sound frightful, worried, before she turns to her mother. "It's really hard."

"I know, honey. Relax. You'll get through this. He can't hurt you, remember that." Tess shoots me a worried look that I completely understand. Aside from the sheer logistics of working our way through this conversation, I don't want to cause the poor girl to break down. She's already been through so much.

But the professional in me can't let it go. "A general idea, maybe? Was he tall? Short? Fat, skinny?"

"He wasn't fat, but he wasn't skinny. Beefy? Is that a good word?"

"Did you ever get an idea of how tall he was?"

"Yeah, he took me to the bathroom. I stood next to him. I reached his shoulder." That would make him roughly six feet tall. "The cabin was always really dark, not just the room I was in. I don't think there was any electricity in there. Just the lanterns. He lit a candle for me when I had to go to the bathroom."

Definitely sounds like a hunting cabin rather than a sort of place someone calls home.

"Do you know anything else about the rest of the cabin? When he took you out of your room, I mean? Did you see anything else?"

"Not really. I mean, I wasn't there for all that long. Just that first night, and the one after it. That was when I got away."

We haven't gotten to that part of my questioning yet, and there are still things I need to know about those first hours after she woke up in a strange place, but this catches my attention and won't let go. I had no idea. "Hang on a second. I wasn't informed of this. When did you escape?"

"I don't know how long it's been, exactly. I didn't know what day it was when I got out, but I'm guessing it was after the second full day because of the light outside the window. It was night when I got out. I took the blankets with me since I couldn't find my coat. I don't know what he did with my backpack, either. But I was still in my clothes. I even had my shoes on. I didn't want to take them off in case I had a chance to run."

Tess barely smothers a sob with a cough. "That was extremely smart," I tell her with a smile. "You're as smart as everybody told me you were." I already know from the tests run after she came in that there was no evidence of sexual assault. Now I know he left her fully dressed while keeping her in the cabin. It's unusual, the absence of that aspect. The same was true with Lila.

"You're sure there was nobody else at the

cabin?" I ask, thinking of her. "Any other voices? A girl, maybe?"

"No. Nobody. He never even really said anything when I saw him. I asked what he wanted from me." Her voice catches before she closes her eyes and lets her head fall against the pillow behind it. "He wouldn't say. That was the worst part."

"I can't imagine how awful it must have been." I wait while she sips her juice before returning to the timeline. "So, you decided to make your escape."

"Yeah. He drove away on maybe the second or third day—I'm a little confused about which day it was—and I got out. There was a sharp, rusty part on the bedframe and I used it to cut the rope he'd tied my wrists with. I wrapped the blankets around me and ran away."

She was out there for days. It's a miracle she survived.

Now, she's here with us, but she's also there. In the past. "I couldn't tell where I was." Her voice is flat as she stares across the room at an enormous arrangement of colorful flowers. "I just kept walking and walking. I tripped and fell and cut my lip, and then I fell down a slope another time. I was afraid to stop. I just had to get as far away as I could."

She runs her free hand under her eyes before lifting a shoulder in a shrug. "I found another cabin that was full of, like, animal bodies and bones and stuff, but it was a roof over my head. So I slept there for a little while during the day and went back out. I figured I'd walk for a little while and if I didn't find anything, I would go back and start off in another direction. But I got lost. It was like in that Blair Witch movie. I was ... so ... scared ..."

She falls against her mother and weeps while clutching her like she's a little girl again, crying over a bad dream. This was no dream. She made it out in one piece, but recovery won't be simple.

I wait silently until she pulls herself together enough to finish her story. "By the time I found the road, I had been awake forever and I never ate anything, so I was too weak to keep going. It was snowing, too. I was so tired. I guess I hoped I'd wake up if I heard a car coming, or that they'd see me and stop. It made sense at the time."

"I might have done the same thing." The

fact is, I can't imagine what she suffered. What she's described takes everything they threw at us during training and multiplies it by ten.

I doubt she has the first idea which direction she traveled in, so I won't bother asking. If she'd had the first clue how to navigate, she wouldn't have spent days wandering in cold, unforgiving woods. It would be an insult if I posed such a question.

Instead, I stand and end the recording. "I'll let you get some rest now. Thank you for talking with me."

"Thank you for rescuing me." She offers a shy smile through her tears. "I'll try to keep thinking about it. If I remember anything else, I'll let you know."

Tess clicks her tongue in a caring, motherly way. "Now, now, I don't want you to force yourself to think back on it."

There's a deep sadness in Camille's eyes when she responds. "I'm not forcing myself. I wish I could stop."

Chapter 32

"How far could she possibly have walked?" Andy looks around the conference room, shrugging. "A little girl like that?"

"Over the course of days?" I counter while the rest of the room watches us silently. I've just finished recounting everything Camille described while Captain Felch scrawled notes on a whiteboard behind me.

"I'm just saying. For all we know, she walked around in circles for days and finally took the right turn that led her to the road."

"Or," one of the other officers interjects, "she could have been walking in a straight line. It's possible. There's hundreds of acres of wooded land out there. A girl on the verge of exhaustion, starving, terrified? It could have been slow going, but it's possible she walked miles and miles in roughly the same direction."

"This is all hypothetical at the moment." As usual, the captain's strong voice fills the room and silences the overlapping voices that have posed questions and theories ever since they learned what Camille shared with me. "Until we get out there, we're not going to know."

He nods at me. "What are we looking at?"

"The Bureau is sending a team that should be here within the hour." It isn't easy staying calm and collected when what I want more than anything is to get out there and find this guy. "We'll have air support, as well, so there will be eyes in the sky looking for this cabin."

"There's plenty of hunting cabins out in those woods," Andy points out. "It could be any one of them."

"We'll have plenty of bodies out there," I remind him. "And we're looking up property records as we speak, so that's covered. As soon as we find the place, we'll know who it belongs to."

"Excuse me." One of the few women in the room raises her hand. Her name is Stephanie, if I remember correctly. "I have a question."

"Let's hear it," I invite. It's rare for the

KATE GABLE

women to speak up. I wish I could say I can't relate to the pressure of being one of the only ones in a room full of men.

"How will we know it's the right cabin? From what you've described, she hasn't given us that much to go on."

"Yes, I realize that," I assure her. "But she described the room she was being held in pretty clearly. We're looking for a room with a metal framed bed—there may or may not still be rope or twine nearby that he used to tie her with. There will be an old-fashioned stove in one corner. No electricity."

"At least, none that he used while she was there," Andy interjects. He always has to interject. Even at a time like this. But he does make a point.

"Sure, that's possible. He might have kept the lights off to keep her unsteady, or to avoid being noticed by anyone near the cabin." I offer the captain a shrug. "It's possible he used this as his residence."

"In other words," Captain Felch announces, "we search every cabin we find. Whether or not they're inhabited."

"And don't forget," I add, "we're looking for a blue vehicle."

Forest of Silence

"Yes, keep an eye out for cabins with a blue vehicle parked nearby." The captain makes a note of that on his whiteboard. It isn't much, but it's all we have to go on.

We exchange a look once the group disperses to prepare for the search, and I can tell he feels my reservations. "I should talk to her again," I murmur as I study the board. Now that everything's laid out in red sharpie, there's no ignoring the way my heart sinks. We're looking for a needle in a haystack.

"It might be too much," he reminds me. "We have to keep her wellbeing in mind."

"Which is why I didn't press any harder than I did." I scrub my hands over my face and groan. "It feels like every step I take forward, I fall back another two steps."

"You need to stop taking all of this on yourself."

"Funny. That's not the first time I've heard that in the past couple of days."

He offers a thin, tired smile. "Well, that just tells me you have plenty of wise people in your life who you need to pay closer attention to."

I can't help laughing softly, mostly at myself.

"Think about it." He waits until I've dropped my hands to my sides. "You found her.

She is alive, and she's going to go home to her family. That's the best result we could hope for."

"The best result we can hope for is to find this guy and stop him."

"Of course, that's what we all want. I'm only asking you not to lose sight of what you've accomplished."

It's not enough. I see what he's saying, but it's not enough. Not until this monster is brought in and put behind bars. "There are still so many questions."

"Let's hear it." He takes a seat at the conference table. "What are you thinking?"

Since there's not much we can do until the team arrives, I'll indulge him. It might help to get everything out of my head, anyway. A brain dump. "For starters, is this the same guy who killed Lila?"

"That's what we're all wondering."

"I don't think it's only a matter of two girls being kidnapped within days of each other. Neither of them were assaulted, for one."

"That is true. They have that in common."

"He left both girls fully dressed, in fact."

"That's right."

"And when I think back on the rough timeline Camille gave me, it fits. The way she described it, she could very well have escaped the night Lila was taken and killed. What if he didn't do it at the cabin?"

"If this is the same guy," he reminds me.

"Yes, yes. If this is the same guy." I wave a dismissive hand before I can stop myself. I don't want to show disrespect, but at times like this, I'm not much interested in technicalities. Not when this all seems to fit together so obviously. "He could have lost control while he was in his car. What if Lila tried to fight back? He used what sounds like chloroform to subdue Camille —what if that wasn't the case with Lila? What if she was awake and alert? That would explain why so little time passed between her disappearance and the discovery of her body."

"So while he was out there disposing of Lila …"

"Exactly. Camille had the chance to get out."

"This is still all a theory."

"Of course yes. But it fits."

"It does. I'm not disagreeing with you. I like the way you think. But until we find proof …"

"I know." The more I think about it, the more sense it makes. It isn't easy to hold myself back when I'm this sure.

"This is what your gut is telling you, isn't it?" he asks with a resigned sigh.

"Yes, my gut is telling me this is much too big a coincidence to only be a coincidence. Unless we have two different people out there taking and killing teenage girls at the same time in the same small town, and what are the odds of that?"

He stands, groaning wearily like his body is resistant. I know the feeling— and it's only going to get worse once we're out in the cold, stomping through snow. "All we have to do now is find the cabin and hope there's evidence tying him to both girls."

There's something else he doesn't need to say. I'm already well aware.

We have to find *him*. Finding the cabin isn't enough. We either have to hope he's there or hope there's something inside that identifies him so we can find him, whoever he is.

I head to my office, where I pull up satellite images of the area where I found Camille. Since I found her on the side of the road, I decide to start scrolling along that side of Route One, assuming she didn't cross the road before deciding to lie down and rest. The woods stretch out for miles, but they thin out the further south

Forest of Silence

I go. The closer to Broken Hill's downtown area.

So it makes sense she was coming from either the north or the east. Otherwise, she would have been able to see how close she was coming to Broken Hill way before she found the road. But in the north and east where the woods are thicker, everything would have looked the same. I wonder what that was like for her. A fifteen-year-old girl, wandering alone. It rained, it snowed. Granted, it sounds like she found the abandoned cabin she stayed in while it rained— she was probably there when Lila was discovered, come to think of it. She was sleeping, wrapped in dirty blankets, while another victim was lying dead not far from Camille's house.

And if my theory is correct, Lila's death was what helped Camille escape. If he hadn't picked her up, he could have gone back to the cabin and strangled Camille, instead.

It's unusual to find a predator like this who doesn't bother sexually assaulting his victims. But he might have, if given the time. That might have been his plan all along. He simply didn't get around to it.

The fact is, this is all guesswork until I have the guy in front of me. In the meantime, all I can do is search for cabins on Google Earth in hopes of making it easier to find it once we're out there.

But we will find it. That much, I'm sure of.

I'm not so sure of what else we'll find.

Chapter 33

I barely feel the cold anymore as I hike through ankle-deep snow along with dozens of officers and agents. We're spread out in a circle three miles wide and working our way in while the whirring of helicopter blades pierces the air. Aside from occasional chatter on the radio I hold in one hand, that's the only sound in the otherwise silent woods.

We've been out here for over an hour, racing the sun. It's one thing to be out here in full daylight— that's treacherous enough, considering the terrain. I've already slipped and almost fallen more than once, and every time I do I imagine what it must have been like for Camille. I'm having a difficult enough time staying on my feet without being terrified my captor would find me if I didn't keep moving. Not to mention how hurried she must have felt thanks to the cold and the weather and her hunger.

The bare branches sway overhead, like bony fingers reaching out from a grave. They must have seemed so much more menacing to the poor kid. Maybe one day, she will fully understand how fortunate she was to make it out in one piece. Just how many things could have gone differently and would have resulted in a different outcome.

There's static on the radio before a voice cuts in. "We have eyes on a structure in the northwest quadrant," someone announces. Probably one of the agents watching from overhead. "I see a team a quarter of a mile further west. Straight ahead, you can't miss it."

"Any cars in the vicinity?" someone asks.

"Negative." No, I doubt we would get that lucky. He might not even be around— after all, Camille escaped. Maybe he's lying low. I hope not, but I have to be realistic.

I hold up a hand to halt the progress of my team and we wait. We're in the northeast quadrant, and eventually would have reached the location in question, but the other team is closer.

Forest of Silence

"The place looks abandoned." I hold the radio to my ear to make sure I'm hearing clearly. "Most of the windows are broken out and there's been plenty of animals taking advantage, by the looks of it."

"Camille Martin described a cabin like that one," I announce on the radio. "It was where she took shelter hours after her escape."

Now, we have a new mission, make it to that cabin and work our way outward. My pulse is racing. This is it. We're finally on to something. She couldn't have gotten far, even running the way she was. It's still slow going out here— and she was in the dark, too. I doubt she could have covered that much ground before finding shelter.

It's another brisk twenty-minute hike before I catch sight of a glow up ahead from a handful of flashlights. Andy is there, and he shakes his head once he sees me. "There's no evidence of her ever being here," he says. "Not that there would be. I mean, the place is wrecked."

I have to see for myself, so I step inside and run my flashlight over the floor before pointing to a spot where it seems like the layers of dust and leaves have been disturbed. "That could have been her," I reason. "Either that, or a very

319

big animal decided to lie down and take a nap."

"You feel good about this?" he asks.

"Are you kidding? Ready to jump out of my skin."

We stepped back outside and he falls in step beside me without saying a word. I don't mind. He's not a bad cop when he's acting like a normal human being. "God, this must have been terrifying," he murmurs as we head north. The helicopter is up ahead, its lights trained on the woods below.

"I can't even imagine," I admit. "And I'm twice her age and I've been trained to take care of myself in the elements. She hasn't."

"You think we have a chance of finding this guy there?"

"Honestly? With all the ruckus? Even if he dared to return after she escaped, he would have to know by now we're on to him."

"At this point, it's just a matter of being able to identify him," he points out.

"That's right."

I catch him smirking my way. "But something tells me you wouldn't mind if we ran into him."

"Would you mind?"

Forest of Silence

"I can't say that I would." His jaw tightens and his eyes go hard. "I think I'd like to get to know him a little better, to tell you the truth."

"I'm afraid you would have to wait your turn."

"Do you think he killed Lila?"

"I absolutely do."

"Me too." He throws an arm in front of me, stopping me before I fall after tripping over a covered root. "Try not to break your neck before we find him, okay?"

"I'll be fine so long as your reflexes are still sharp." We share a brief smile but soon turn serious again, sweeping the area with our eyes but getting nowhere.

Until ...

"Wait a minute!" I hear Andy calling out behind me but I'm not about to stop once I recognize a sloped, sagging roof hidden inside a densely packed cluster of trees. If this were spring or summer, the place would be completely hidden by thick leaves, making it the perfect place to stash a victim or two.

This is it. I feel it in my bones. There is no vehicle parked nearby but there are tire tracks visible in the snow. He's been here recently.

"I found something!" I call into the radio

while Andy joins me and starts looking through the grimy windows. I use my flashlight to catch the attention of the nearby team members before joining him.

"Look at this." Excitement throbs in his voice as he steps aside, pointing into the window. "Metal bed frame, stove in the corner." Yes, both are visible through the dirty window. The room is dark like the rest of the cabin, and easily close enough that Camille could have made it to shelter before the rain started to fall overnight. "I think this is it."

I draw my weapon and make sure it's ready before circling the cabin. He could be somewhere nearby, watching while we descend upon his hideout. For some twisted animals like the one we're dealing with, that's what it's all about. Knowing they can pull the strings and make law enforcement rush around in a frenzy.

It takes nothing to kick the door in. "Federal officer!" I shout, the pistol held in front of me while I swing the flashlight around with my other hand.

"It looks empty," Andy mutters behind me. He's right. There's nobody here. Either he knew we were onto him, or he left before we could get too close.

Forest of Silence

Right away, I head for the room we studied from outside. It's smaller than I imagined, only eight by eight at the most, and the bed takes up almost the entire wall it sits against. I take note of the stained mattress but it's the bed frame I'm most interested in. She described a rusty, broken bit of metal which she used to cut her ropes.

"Look at this!" There's no hope of keeping the excitement out of my voice as I wave Andy into the room and train the flashlight on the jagged metal, where bits of blue nylon fiber hang free.

"Remind me again of the fibers found in Lila's skin?" Andy mutters.

"Blue nylon."

This is it. I'll wait for the forensic team to take care of that while we examine the rest of the cabin and wait for the team to catch up. There isn't much to see— a single room serves as living room and makeshift kitchen. There's a hot plate and a coffee maker on a chipped, stained counter. The sink is rusted— and he turns one of the taps and clear water runs out.

"I wouldn't be surprised if this was only his den," he observes, and I'm inclined to agree when considering the condition of the place. An animal's den.

"Yes, he could have a permanent residence elsewhere." I'm not sure, though, since there's plenty of dry goods in the pantry and— surprise — the interior of the old-fashioned, empty refrigerator is cool, if not cold. "There was a generator outside, wasn't there?" I ask.

"Yeah, there was. He must have turned it off." That solves that mystery.

Some of the floorboards sag and groan at the slightest bit of weight as Andy steps on them, and something skitters in the cabinet under the sink when I take a look inside. I quickly close the door before there's a chance for us to become acquainted. Yet another thing the forensics team can deal with. I'm not sure I could handle an attack by a rabid raccoon at this point.

"Alexis!" It doesn't hit me right away that Andy used my first name instead of calling me Agent Forrest. It doesn't register when compared to the excitement in his voice. "You have got to see this! Get in here!"

I only thought I was prepared for what I might find today. Never in my wildest imaginings did I figure on uncovering a room like this. At one point, it must have served as a bedroom.

Forest of Silence

In fact, there's still a cot in the corner he could very well have used.

Because who wouldn't want to sleep surrounded by their trophies?

At first, I'm too stunned to speak. It's enough for me to sweep the flashlight's beam over the walls, which have been papered in newspaper clippings. Photos.

And more. A strangled sob escapes me when I realize there's a braid pinned to the wall, like it was cut straight from a girl's head. She had red hair. Next to it is a colorized newspaper photo— and it's no surprise to see the smiling, freckled face girl had long, red hair.

There are so many more. So very many.

"Oh. Oh, no."

I don't have the chance to ask Andy what that's all about before he's forcibly pushing me from the room. "You need to go. You don't need this."

"Huh? What are you talking about? Get off me!"

What a surprise. He doesn't listen. "I am telling you, Agent Forrest." He takes me by the shoulders and looks me square in the eye. "You do not need to be in there right now. Let the forensics team do their job."

KATE GABLE

I hear them approaching, too, I hear their engines and their voices. I hear the whir of the helicopter blades. More than anything, I hear the drum beat of my heart in my ears. "What's in there? What did you see?"

He glances over his shoulder, then turns back to me. And I know before he's opened his mouth. I know because I recognize the look on his face. I've seen it so many times, just never from him until now.

Pity. He's looking at the sister of the murdered girl.

"One of those articles ..." He swallows hard. "It was about your sister. It was about Maddie."

Chapter 34

I'm numb. And it isn't the cold making me lose touch with my body. It's the screaming in my head. The part of me that will not allow me to accept what's on that wall.

I had to see it for myself. No way could I have gone on Andy's word alone. He gave up and stepped aside with a look on his face that got a simple message across, *Don't say I didn't warn you.*

And even as I stared at my sister's smiling face, I still couldn't believe it. I had seen those very pictures the newspaper printed more times than I can count. There were three in particular the media used most frequently once Maddie's case went from a tragic abduction and murder and turned to a case of a parent's need for revenge. Once Dad opened fire on those courthouse steps, this story blew up in a big way. National exposure.

Seeing those pictures again brought it all back. A radiant Maddie, all dolled up for her freshman dance in a light pink dress she promised she would give me when my time came. She was buried in that dress. There's another, one which used to be of the two of us standing in front of our Christmas tree. I was cropped out, of course. And the third was her yearbook photo. She still had her braces when it was taken. They were only removed a month before she died.

Was murdered.

I still see those images in front of me as I pace outside the cabin, lost in a flood of memories and the ever present sense of being in a nightmare. The sort of nightmare you're glad to wake up from, then return to as soon as you go back to sleep. I've always hated those, to the point where I got in the habit of staying awake after a nightmare just in case it wasn't finished with me yet.

I can't wake up from this one. I only wish I could.

Is it possible? It's been twenty years. Twenty

years, and the man convicted of my sister's murder has sat in prison all that time. Is it the right man? My stomach clenches and I have to force a few deep breaths to fight back an overwhelming wave of nausea. Is an innocent man rotting in prison while the man responsible for killing my beautiful, brilliant sister has been free to kill again and again?

I'm thirty years old. I have a doctorate. I'm an FBI agent. And all I want is my mommy and daddy to tell me everything is going to be okay. The thing is, they are the last people who need to hear this right now. Oh, what is it going to do to Dad? The question makes me bend at the waist, gripping my knees. Trying to breathe. He shot that man. He tried to kill him and said goodbye to life as we all knew it.

And the man could be innocent.

Captain Felch finds me fighting for air. There's no need to ask what's wrong with me. No doubt he saw the trophy wall with his own eyes. Either that, or Andy blabbed to him. "Alexis." He places a hand on my back, and it occurs to me this is the second time in less than an hour someone has called me by my first name. "You don't have to be here."

"Are you kidding? This is exactly where I

need to be." I blurt out a thin laugh before standing upright. "I mean, where do I go? What do I do? I can't go home to my mom, since she'll know something's wrong as soon as she sees me."

"I am deeply sorry. I wish there were something I could say. We're going to find him. There's too much evidence here for this to go any other way."

I barely hear him over the roaring in my ears. "My father went to prison over what he did."

"I know."

"There were people out there calling him a hero. I saw it on the news. They said they would have done the same thing. There was even a petition saying he shouldn't be imprisoned for doing what any parent would do."

"There are a lot of people who feel that way when it comes to things like this."

"But it was for nothing." I hold my head in my hands as the repercussions unfold in my imagination. "This would break him. It would break both of them, him and my mom. What if Maddie's killer was on the loose all this time? That's the one thing that gave her peace, you know," I point out, laughing bitterly at the memory. "Knowing that monster was behind bars and could never destroy another family."

I point through the open door of the cabin. "How many of those articles were from after Maddie? It's been twenty years. Who knows how many more he's killed?"

"And you couldn't have stopped him."

"I know that's supposed to make me feel better, but it doesn't."

"I'm only hoping to give you a little perspective. Nobody knew. A jury convicted that man. Even his own lawyers thought he did it." When I shoot him a quizzical look, he shrugs. "You think I didn't research the case when you came to town? I may not have been here at the time, but the internet is vast."

"That's just it. His lawyers thought he did it. They didn't even try. Oh, this keeps getting worse."

He slides his gloved hands into his coat pockets and sighs. "One thing at a time. We have to catch this guy."

"Oh, nothing can stop me," I assure him. "You think I was obsessed before?"

"One thing at a time." The team begins leaving with boxes of evidence, and on top of one of the boxes is a handful of framed photos unlike the ones tacked to the wall. I pull on a fresh pair of gloves before reaching into the box and pulling out a couple of the frames.

One of the photos features a man wearing waders, standing in water up to his knees and holding up an enormous fish. "I recognize this place," the captain murmurs. "Should only be a few miles from here, along the river."

"Wait." I hold it closer to my face, but it's already getting dark out here so I use my flashlight to study the image more closely.

There goes that tingle in the back of my neck. Right on schedule. "I know this man."

"You what?"

"I don't know him personally, not that way. But I've seen him. I've spoken to him." I just can't remember when or where. I recognize the red ball cap and the wire rimmed glasses. I've seen them before. But I've seen so many people lately. At the bookstore? Somewhere else in town? *Think, Alexis!*

Then it hits me. "Hawthorne! He was at Hawthorne!"

"You're sure?"

"The handyman! He gave me directions!"

I look around wildly, dropping the photo in favor of running to one of the black sedans used

Forest of Silence

by the agents who drove out here. "I need this!"
I shout. "Immediately! Keys!" I don't know who
throws them to me. I only know I catch them
deftly and throw myself behind the wheel. I
barely catch a glimpse of Captain Felch
watching me as I speed away, probably driving
too fast for the conditions but not caring much.

He was there. He was right in front of me!
And I thanked him for his help! Did he know
who I was, why I was there? Has he been
laughing at me all this time? Or did he take it as
a close call, maybe tell himself he needs to be
more careful? By this time, Lila was dead, and
Camille had run away from his cabin. I'm
surprised he was still in the area at all.

And oh, there are so many kids at that
school. Did she know him? Did she recognize
him from around campus when he picked her
up? She probably thought he was someone she
could trust. Maybe she was on her way to the
bus station one town over and he offered to give
her a ride. I can see it playing out in my head as
I swing a hard right turn that places me on
Route One. *It's a cold night. Why don't I give you a
ride?"* I slam my hand against the wheel, furious
and heartbroken. She thought she could
trust him.

333

KATE GABLE

How did he gain Maddie's trust?

I can't think about that now, but that's all my mind keeps wanting to return to. Maddie. My beautiful sister. Did he gain her trust? Was he living nearby at the time? Was he already using the cabin? Or did he only collect his clippings back then, with no place to put them? So many questions, most of which will probably never get answered. But I'll never stop asking them.

Right away, the officer at the guard house shakes his head when I give him my name. "I'm sorry, but—"

"There is no doubt about this. We've identified the prime suspect as someone who works in this school. Now you let me through, and you call the president's office to tell him I am on my way. Unless you want me to have you arrested."

Needless to say, he allows me through, and it takes all the self-control I possess to maintain a slow speed as I drive to the lot reserved for administrators. I've barely got the car in park before I cut the engine and dash up the walkway and through the front door.

President Winters meets me there, looking flustered and deeply put off. "What is this all about?" he demands. "You have a suspect?"

"Yes, and I need you to give me all the infor-

334

mation you have on him. I met him the day I went to the security office. He was carrying a toolbox and wearing blue coveralls and a red ball cap. I didn't get his name."

He falls back half a step, his eyes darting over my face from behind those glasses of his. "And you're sure of this?"

"There was a photo of him— there's no time for this!" I insist. "I have to find this man. You must help me."

"Alright. Alright." He holds up both hands, then motions for me to follow him. We haven't yet stepped through his office door before he's shouting to his assistant. "Meg? I need you to pull everything we have on Harvey Steinman, and I mean I need it minutes ago."

Chapter 35

"He hasn't been here in the past two days?" They must be joking. Or I misheard them. "You're sure of this?"

The kindly security officer I met down at his office that fateful day offers a pained shrug. "I'm sorry, but there's no record of him using his badge in the past two days."

"And he was on the schedule," President Winters informs me while typing frantically on his keyboard. "I'm looking at the notes from the administrative office and it looks like someone tried to reach out and get in touch with him, but the calls went unanswered."

Two days. He's had two days head start. "But who is he? That's what I need to know."

"Here you go." Meg rushes in holding a

folder. "This is everything we have on him."

"Do you mind if I make a call?" I'm already pulling my phone from my pocket—the question comes more from habit than anything else. I'm hardly thinking straight at the moment.

Two days. He could be two days away by now. He could be anywhere. What tipped him off? He might have sensed something. That I was getting closer.

Was he watching me in town all this time? Did he follow my progress around campus? For all I know, he could have visited the bookstore while I was there. He could've watched me having dinner with Mitch at the pub. I would never have thought to pay attention to him. He was the sort of person who could easily fade into the background, which I'm sure is by design. You can't afford to be noticed when your favorite pastime involves kidnapping and murder.

Andy picks up on the first ring. "Forrest?"

"Are you at the station?"

"Yeah, thawing out."

"I need you to run a check for me. The name is Harvey Steinman." I spell the name out before continuing. "And check it against the records for the cabin."

"Harvey Steinman? That's not the name on the title."

"Just look him up for me." I rattle off the Social Security number he provided on his paperwork, along with the date of birth. Then I wait for a few moments that feel like an eternity.

"There's nobody coming up for that. No Harvey Steinman with that social or date of birth."

"Search just the social, then."

A moment later, there's a groan. "That number belonged to a Herbert Steinman, but ... he passed away in the late nineties."

"What was the name on the cabin?"

"David Pierce. I was researching him when you called."

"Have you found anything?"

"Negative."

Meanwhile, three pairs of eyes gaze hopefully at me. "One thing's obvious, everything he provided here was fabricated." Meg's shoulders sink. Winters falls back in his chair. His face is slack with dismay. They opened the gates and welcomed the wolf inside, where the sheep were waiting.

"I'll search DMV records for both names,"

Andy suggests. "We might be able to find his vehicle."

"Yes, do that. Thank you. Keep me posted."

"Hey, Agent Forrest." Andy pauses before murmuring, "We're going to find him."

Will we, though? When the man has been running free for at least twenty years? There were articles in that room older than my sister's, the newsprint so yellowed and brittle, it might have crumbled at the first touch. He's been getting away with this for a very long time.

And I had him. I had him right in front of me. We spoke. And I had no idea.

It turns out you can be in the presence of a serial killer and not know it. So many people tell themselves they would know, that something deep down inside would tip them off. I can now say with full certainty that is false. Sometimes, monsters hide in plain sight, and they whistle and carry a toolbox while they do it. All the while, they're strolling around their hunting grounds, looking for their next victim.

And now he's gone, and we don't have the first idea who to look for.

And there were so many articles. So many lives.

He's not going to stop until someone stops

him. You don't kidnap and murder countless girls over the course of decades and suddenly decide to stop.

Someone's going to put an end to this.

And while I know I can't solve all the world's problems, I am certainly going to do my best to solve this one.

Run all you want. I'm going to catch you.

Thank for you reading Forest of Silence. Can't wait to find out what happens to Alexis next? **Grab Forest of Shadows now!**

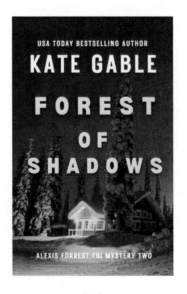

Forest of Silence

When she finds out that the man convicted of killing her sister may be innocent, FBI agent and forensic psychologist Alexis Forrest goes on the search for the real culprit. Evidence of her sister's murder was found in a remote cabin, along with traces of dozens more young women. A serial killer has been stalking these woods for decades and he's still out there.

Alexis had returned to Broken Hill, the snowy New England town where she grew up, to investigate another case. But after finding the serial killer's cabin with evidence of other victims, she will do anything to track him down.

Meanwhile, a family is torn apart when their son goes missing while they're on a family vacation nearby. He disappears while sledding right outside of his Airbnb. The sled is found but the boy is gone. With a huge blizzard blowing in, Alexis must fight against nature and man to find the boy before all of the evidence of who took him and what happened to him is buried.

Will Alexis be able to find the boy in time? Can she find out who killed her sister before the serial killer claims another victim?

1-click Forest of Shadows now!

If you enjoyed this book, please don't forget to leave a review on Amazon and Goodreads! Reviews help me find new readers.

If you have any issues with anything in the book or find any typos, please email me at Kate@kategable.com. Thank you so much for reading!

Also check out my other bestselling and 3 time Silver Falchion award winning series, **Girl Missing.**

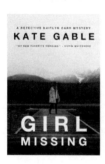

When her 13-year-old sister vanishes on her way back from a friend's house, Detective Kaitlyn Carr must confront demons from her own past in order to bring her sister home.

The small mountain town of Big Bear Lake is only three hours away but a world away from her life in Los Angeles. It's the place she grew up and the place that's plagued her with lies, death and secrets.

Forest of Silence

As Kaitlyn digs deeper into the murder that she is investigating and her sister's disappearance, she finds out that appearances are misleading and few things are what they seem.

A murderer is lurking in the shadows and the more of the mystery that Kaitlyn unspools the closer she gets to danger herself.

Can Kaitlyn find the killer and solve the mystery of her sister's disappearance before it's too late?

What happens when someone else is taken?

1-click Girl Missing now!

About Kate Gable

Kate Gable loves a good mystery that is full of suspense. She grew up devouring psychological thrillers and crime novels as well as movies, tv shows and true crime.

Her favorite stories are the ones that are centered on families with lots of secrets and lies as well as many twists and turns. Her novels have elements of psychological suspense, thriller, mystery and romance.

Kate Gable lives near Palm Springs, CA with her husband, son, a dog and a cat. She has spent more than twenty years in Southern California and finds inspiration from its cities, canyons, deserts, and small mountain towns.

She graduated from University of Southern California with a Bachelor's degree in Mathematics. After pursuing graduate studies in mathematics, she switched gears and got her MA in Creative Writing and English from Western New Mexico University and her PhD in Education from Old Dominion University.

Writing has always been her passion and obsession. Kate is also a USA Today Bestselling author of romantic suspense under another pen name.

Write her here:

Kate@kategable.com

Check out her books here:

www.kategable.com

Sign up for my newsletter:

https://www.subscribepage.com/
kategableviplist

Join my Facebook Group:

https://www.facebook.com/groups/
833851020557518

Bonus Points: Follow me on BookBub and
Goodreads!

https://www.bookbub.com/authors/kate-gable

https://www.goodreads.com/author/show/
21534224.Kate_Gable

amazon.com/Kate-Gable/e/B095XFCLL7

facebook.com/KateGableAuthor

bookbub.com/authors/kate-gable

instagram.com/kategablebooks

tiktok.com/@kategablebooks

Also by Kate Gable

**Detective Kaitlyn Carr Psychological
Mystery series**
Girl Missing (Book 1)
Girl Lost (Book 2)
Girl Found (Book 3)
Girl Taken (Book 4)
Girl Forgotten (Book 5)
Gone Too Soon (Book 6)
Gone Forever (Book 7)
Whispers in the Sand (Book 8)

Girl Hidden (FREE Novella)

**Detective Charlotte Pierce Psychological
Mystery series**

Forest of Silence

Last Breath
Nameless Girl
Missing Lives
Girl in the Lake